VIEW FROM

by Charles Fall

This story is the sequel to *Death Comes To The Dale*. As such I would urge any reader to tackle that first. Nevertheless, *View From The Edge* has been carefully written as a stand-alone book so as to provide enough of the backstory within. It sees David Tanner, Secret Service officer, having to return to Wharfedale for six months to closely monitor a potentially unstable individual who is needed by GCHQ to work on British cyber security. As Tanner's MI5 boss, John Dawson, succinctly puts it:

'It's a no-brainer, David. Your job. Just make sure that nobody ends up dead this time.'

Again it begins….

CHAPTER 1   THE FIRST WEEK IN JANUARY

Jonathan Maxim stood in front of the full-length mirror
applying red lipstick to his boyish lips. He swept his hand
from left to right across his forehead to tidy his short black
hair and then stepped back to admire himself in the mirror.
He liked what he saw, especially the pencil-thin black dress
trimmed at the collar and cuffs with white lace. It reminded
him of his mother, but she was gone now, both physically
and mentally, no trace of her any more in his own brain's
identity. The interrogations and the treatment since her
death had seen to that.

A key turned in the locked door behind him and the two
familiar men entered the room. Both were dressed in what
looked like standard male nurse uniforms, blue in colour.
One held the door open and beckoned. Neither spoke.
Jonathan knew the routine all too well by now. It was four
o'clock in the afternoon and that meant it was time to talk
to Doctor Davis yet again. This had gone on for months and
he had lost track of time, what with the endless questioning,
psychological assessments and changes to the anti-
psychotic drugs they were feeding him. At least the good
doctor pretended to have his best interests at heart, whereas
his less than friendly MI5 interrogators incessantly
demanded that he provide them with the minutest details
about the last eight years, the part he'd played in his
father's covert work, the killing of the two MI5 officers, the

deaths at Scargill Cottage, everything! GCHQ experts took their turn too. They endlessly tried to prise out from him his cyber secrets. How could he do what they themselves could not? Yes, he had studied computer science at Cambridge for two years, but, more importantly, he had been self-taught from the age of ten and regarded them as amateurs. To Jonathan, their questions were inane and none-too-bright. What is more, he knew that these geeks needed his brain, but that they were frightened of him too. Was he a cold-blooded killer or just a victim of circumstance? No matter how many questions MI5 asked, they couldn't tell which.

'Come in,' shouted Davis as the three men approached his office door down a long battleship-grey corridor. Jonathan glanced up at the camera staring down at him. Cameras were everywhere in the clinic. They entered the office and Jonathan took his usual seat opposite Doctor Stuart Davis, senior psychiatrist and Head of the Latham Clinic, which was, in reality, a secret UK Government establishment two miles south of Douglas on the Isle of Man. The two nurses, or guards, depending on your point of view, left the room and waited outside.

'You are a brave man, doctor. There are always at least two MI5s in the room with me when I get my daily interrogation, and I am often handcuffed. Mind you, there is the two-way mirror of course.'

Jonathan licked his lips as he glanced towards the wall to his left. Davis looked down at his notes and then across the desk at his patient.

'Well, Jonathan, you have been here for some fifteen weeks and we have completed our assessment. Today I shall tell you what I think. I use the word think, rather than know, because I am aware of how clever you are and realise that you could be fooling me, at least to an extent. My report to MI5 is full of caveats, disclaimers as you might say.'

'Do carry on, doctor,' said Jonathan.

Davis stared coldly into Maxim's eyes and made a series of statements, stated with a certainty he did not possess.

'At the age of fifteen you were diagnosed as mildly schizophrenic. This worsened when you were at Cambridge and in your twenties when you worked alongside your late father, some activities clearly being outside the law. You have shown signs of violence, sometimes extreme, particularly when failing to take your anti-psychotic medication. You were responsible for your own father's death and partly responsible for the death of at least three other men and your own mother. You remain a schizophrenic, but that diagnosis is somewhat simplistic, undermined by a boyish charm coupled with a brilliance typical of someone with Asperger's syndrome. Going

3

forward, I do not regard you as an inherently dangerous individual, so long as you are monitored closely, and appropriate medication is taken on a permanent basis. You no longer have a dual identity, though persist in wearing women's clothing reminiscent of your mother. You are a heterosexual transvestite, although the term asexual may be more appropriate. I have made MI5 aware of my conclusions in full detail and the risk that you may still pose.'

Jonathan Maxim smiled, shook his head and tutted.

'Dear doctor. Hardly a glowing recommendation to the British Secret Service! You do know that they want me to work for them but that I won't work for them if they keep me in this asylum of yours!'

He realised that he had shouted. He relaxed and smiled again. Davis appeared nervous for the first time.

'Well, doctor, you say that I am at least partly responsible for the deaths of five people. No charges have been brought against me. Why? People ended up dead because they tried to kill me. As for my mother, she was shot by an MI5 officer when trying to save her beloved son. So, I have never been to court, and I have never been charged, because there is no proof of intent to kill, except in self-defence. Let's face it, I am in this clinic of yours because I am judged to be a schizophrenic. The law can justify putting me away. I accept that, but they are not going to put me away, are they?'

Davis glanced at the two-way mirror.

'What you know, your expertise, and what you can do for them, Jonathan, must be extremely important, but I am not privy to such considerations. If it were my decision? But it isn't. You will be leaving the clinic, and soon. I have been told by both MI5 and GCHQ that you have been very cooperative so far. MI5 are pleased with you, but there will be restrictions on your freedom from now on, forever, Jonathan. You will never be rid of the watchers.'

'Never is a long time, doctor, never is a long time.'

Davis gathered his notes, nodded towards the mirror to his right, stood up and, without uttering another word, left the room. A door situated in the wall behind the doctor's desk immediately opened and a tall middle-aged besuited man entered and sat down opposite Maxim. Jonathan had never seen him before but his demeanour exuded status and self-confidence. The man folded his arms and leaned back in the chair, appearing completely relaxed.

'You have done well here, Jonathan, since those rather unfortunate events in Yorkshire. GCHQ are positively excited about the information that you have given them. A step change in our security, they tell me. Praise indeed! They would like more, of course. They estimate that you have shown them ninety percent and say that it's enough for them to start to replicate your abilities, how you hide on the web, how you hack invisibly, how you transfer data around, and how you make what you do untraceable. GCHQ is impressed, and that takes a lot of doing. So, Jonathan, for the time being at least, you are untouchable, an asset who must be treasured, but with a restriction or two.'

'Who are you?' asked Maxim. 'I'm going to guess that you're Tanner's boss, an MI5 high-up. Is Mister Tanner well?'

The man ignored the question.

'We have felt obliged to drain your accounts, including those here on the island, well, the ones we could trace, but so far have been unable to legitimately touch those in your sister's name. So, in theory you are penniless, at least temporarily, whereas Mrs Sally Henshaw remains considerably well off. She has been informed that you will be returning to Wharfedale and will be here tomorrow to collect you.'

Maxim instinctively clapped his hands, much to the amazement of senior MI5 officer John Dawson.

'You will be allowed to return to your cottage where you will work on our behalf. You are clearly unsuited to

6

working in an office environment with other people. You will be monitored constantly and visited from time to time. Your technical equipment will be limited and linked directly to GCHQ. No other hardware facilities will be available to you. Your sister will be responsible for your well-being. Any breach of our conditions, set out in a document I shall give you, will result in the prosecution of you and your sister under the Official Secrets Act or any other appropriate act. In your case, this would lead to confinement for life in a mental institution.'

Maxim nodded his agreement, almost mockingly.

'And there is one more condition,' added Dawson.

'And what is that?' asked Maxim.

'You will be GPS chipped. A simple procedure, this evening. We will know where you are 24/7, Jonathan, 24/7, from now on, for all time. You will be state of the art, not on the market yet, way ahead of your time.'

Dawson laughed and waited for Maxim to explode but no explosion came.

'Just like a labrador,' was the quiet reply.

To Jonathan Maxim, he had won the game. He was leaving this prison.

CHAPTER 2

The three cars, the first a hearse, the second a small
Mercedes and the third a large Range Rover, slowly
travelled along the winding road from Buckden into
Hubberholme as snow began to fall on a winter's Sunday
morning. They parked outside the churchyard, opposite The
George. It was only eight o'clock and the small hamlet of
Hubberholme had yet to show any sign of life. Four men,
dressed in army uniform, emerged quickly from the Range
Rover and removed a coffin from the hearse. Seemingly
with little effort, they carried it into the churchyard and
across to the far side where a grave had been dug the night
before by these same men. They then brought a second
coffin, identical to the first, to the graveside. They slowly
lowered both coffins into the grave and then stepped back
against the wall behind them and stood to attention.

At that same moment, four people emerged from the
Mercedes. The first two were Jonathan Maxim and Sally
Henshaw, his twin sister. The other two were John Dawson
and a priest. A minute later they were all stood by the
grave, where the priest read words from the bible and
conducted a short funeral service as requested by Sally. She
looked stunning as she always did, a tall slim woman of
twenty-eight, with long golden hair, dressed in black, with
a single red rose pinned to her coat lapel. Her face showed
no sign of emotion. Her brother, standing to her left, was

dressed in his own father's SAS uniform, and was in floods of tears, crying loudly with no embarrassment at all.

As the priest said his final 'amen', Sally removed the rose from her lapel, kissed it and tossed it into the grave.

'It's time to stop crying now, Jonny,' she said firmly.

Jonathan's face changed in that instant. The tears were no more.

'It's been a lovely ceremony, Sal,' he said. 'Mother and father will be so pleased, to be together.'

The two siblings walked with the priest back to their car, while Dawson said a few words to the soldiers who, within five minutes, had filled the unmarked grave with earth. Two minutes later, the three cars left Hubberholme.

Unknown to anyone, except his boss John Dawson, the whole scene had been witnessed through binoculars from only a hundred yards away.

'Welcome back to Wharfedale, Jonathan.'

David Tanner, the MI5 officer responsible for the capture of Jonathan only a few months before, had been given the task of monitoring Maxim for what his boss had said would be 'an indeterminate period, depending on what happens'.

He was not a happy man. His recall to London, after exile in Catterick of all places, had been exactly what he had wanted, what he had schemed for, what he had risked his life for. He still bore the scars of Peter Wilson's death and would have been content to see Maxim locked away for good but, underneath, the feelings of self-guilt still invaded his thoughts and dreams far too often. Nevertheless, he understood Maxim and Sally Henshaw better than any other MI5 officer. He knew Wharfedale and had contacts with local police. As Dawson had said:

'It's a no-brainer, David. Your job. Just make sure that nobody ends up dead this time.'

Tanner walked briskly to his car and then drove slowly down the dale a few miles to Kettlewell where he'd rented a small holiday cottage for the duration. He spent the rest of the morning and afternoon going through Doctor Davis's psychological report on Maxim, MI5 and GCHQ's documentation and his own report on the Wilson debacle. Dawson had emphasised how important Maxim was to GCHQ and what his expertise could bring to UK security and, eventually, to possible MI6 covert cyber ops. He was a golden asset, but one that must be watched like a hawk.

That evening Sally Henshaw, owner and landlady of The Inn in Buckden, received the phone call she was expecting and the next morning Tanner drove her the three miles up to Scargill Cottage, situated a mile beyond Cray, to meet with her brother. The idea was to avoid any confrontation between the two men by having Sally present.

Sally led Tanner straight into the cottage and immediately left, through the kitchen, to Jonathan's own room, with its en suite facilities and technical equipment, less now than Tanner remembered from his last fateful visit. Maxim had watched them on screen as they approached the cottage, via the surveillance cameras that were still functioning. He was standing in the middle of the room with his arms folded, dressed in black jeans and sweater but with his face fully made up.

'I was wondering when you'd show up, MI5,' he said, sharply, 'do we have any outstanding business to attend to?'

'No, Jonathan,' came the reply, 'you didn't kill me, and I didn't kill you. We move on.'

'But you did kill my mother!'

'Self-defence, something you claim to know a lot about!'

'Stop it, both of you!' shouted Sally. 'We all know what happened and we all blame who we want to blame. It's over. Jonny, you're back here with me. That's what you wanted. That's what you needed. But Mister Tanner has a job to do and, for all our sakes, we have to let him do it.'

'OK, Sal,' said Maxim, quietly, and retreated to his desk chair.

'Thank you, Mrs Henshaw.' Tanner sounded sincere.

He spent the next half hour re-iterating the rules of the game to Maxim who became very bored, very quickly, but did pay attention to the salient points. Tanner would visit him probably twice a week, at any time of his own choosing, to check that all was well in the cottage, and would receive reports from GCHQ and MI5 regarding the work that Maxim was doing.

'And what about this annoying GPS chip under the skin behind my left shoulder?' asked Maxim. 'You know all about that I suppose.'

'Yes,' replied Tanner. 'GCHQ, MI5 and me, we all know where you are every minute of the day, in real time. I can track you any time on my smartphone. You know the rules. Confined to barracks, within a few hundred metres, say. Realise this. If you step outside these boundaries, you will be stopped, and back to the clinic you go. All your needs and wants will be catered for by your sister. But there can be light at the end of the tunnel. If you do a good job for us and don't mess up, your case will be reviewed in six months. Things can change, Jonathan, it's down to you.'

Maxim nodded. Six months didn't seem so bad. Well, not today at any rate.

For the next week or so Jonathan stayed indoors virtually all day, interacting with GCHQ experts and identifying overseas hacker sites unknown to the Secret Service. He was enjoying himself. He saw Sally every day and Tanner had only turned up on two evenings to annoy him and interrupt his online chess games. They too were monitored closely by GCHQ. The first thing that he'd realised on his return to Scargill Cottage was that the black SUV had not returned. As expected, he had no car, but there was still the quad bike. For fun, he'd raced it up and down the long drive a few times.

And then, one morning, for no apparent reason, he woke up very depressed and angry. He didn't wash, he didn't shave, and he didn't do his make-up. Why should he be confined to barracks? This was ridiculous, an insult. He wasn't dangerous. None of this had been his fault. He threw on his jeans and sweater and stormed out of the cottage. He stared at the wood to his right where his mother and father's bodies had lain and ran haphazardly into it. Exiting the wood, he saw a man in the distance. He recognised the portly figure instantly. It was his neighbour Fred Denby, out walking with his shotgun, on the lookout for rabbits no doubt. Maxim gave a yelp of excitement and raced towards him. Approaching the farmer at speed, he flung his arms around him, with a 'oh, it's so good to see you, Fred!'

'Bloody hell, Jon, you're back!' came the shocked reply. 'The rumour I heard was that you were banged up for life.

Sad about your mother, Jon. A lovely lady. I kept people away from the cottage, after you, er, disappeared, like Mrs Henshaw wanted. Ghouls, the lot of 'em. A pop from my shotgun sent them packing though. And a few home-made Keep Out signs. Anyway, do you fancy a bit of a shoot? Rabbits, pigeons, I could do with the company.'

Jonathan laughed until he cried.

'You could do with company! Yes, Fred, great, but I don't have my shotgun anymore.'

'Aw, don't worry about that, Jon, you can borrow my two-two rifle if you fancy. It'll make it more of a challenge.'

The two 'friends' walked the few hundred yards to Scargill Farm, where Fred dug out the two-two. For the following two hours Fred nattered incessantly about how hard up he was, how he was too old for farming these days, and how the horses were letting him down currently, while Jonathan Maxim had target practice with a field full of rabbits. Seven rabbits died that morning.

That lunchtime, David Tanner received an emailed message detailing Jonathan Maxim's movement away from Scargill Cottage. The last line read:

'Of no real concern. Within stated limits.'

The next morning Sally Henshaw drove from Buckden into Kettlewell to buy some supplies for Jonathan. The village only had a few small shops but enough for her to get the Yorkshire Tea, bread and milk, fruit, tins and ready meals that were Jonny's standard fare. He didn't like cooking and ate sparingly. As she placed her carrier bags in the boot of her new red SUV, she glanced across the street to see a familiar face crossing the road. It was David Tanner. Unseen, she set off back up the dale to Cray and fifteen minutes later brought the car to a halt next to the mud splattered quadbike sat on the long tarmac drive outside Scargill Cottage. As she opened the boot, her brother was already running towards her.

'Let me give you a hand, Sis,' he said enthusiastically.

'You seem jolly today,' replied Sally with a smile. 'Thought you were getting a bit down, maybe. Is the work you're doing going well? Keeping you busy? Interesting?'

'Oh, the work's OK. Pretty straightforward stuff. Anyway, it's secret,' he added with a laugh. 'No, the good thing is that I went for a bit of a walk yesterday and came across Fred Denby. Same as usual. Moaned about being hard up, even after all the money we've given him.'

Sally gave her brother an admonishing look of suspicion.

'Oh, no worries, Sal, but any chance of giving me some money? Fred could be useful, as before, in keeping an eye on the place and discouraging walkers, and maybe helping with one or two things.'

'What things, Jonny?'

'Oh, don't be like that, Sal. Nothing specific, but I don't have any cash now. What if you were too busy in the pub, for instance, and I needed something. Well, I can't go anywhere, but Fred can.'

'What a load of tosh, Jonny! However, you probably do need cash, just in case.'

'What do you mean, just in case?'

Sally ignored the question.

'I got your supplies down in Kettlewell, and who do you think I saw crossing the road in front of me only twenty minutes ago?'

Jonny thought a second and then smiled.

'Mister MI5?'

'Yes, Mister MI5.'

'So that's where he is.'

Jonathan carried the three carrier bags into the cottage followed by his sister. She put the food away and then made him beans on toast to have with a pot of tea. He checked his emails.

'GCHQ is still asleep,' he joked as he tucked into his breakfast.

'Remember,' said Sally seriously, 'we're lucky to be back here in Wharfedale. It is our home now. I have Tom at The Inn and I've got you up here. You two are my life. You must be careful, Jonny, and don't break any of the rules.'

She went through to the kitchen and returned with a glass of water and two tablets.

'Now, take these,' she said.

Jonathan Maxim took his anti-psychotic medication. He was feeling happier today than he had for months. He was back home, his work was better than expected, and he had a friend now, even though it was only Fred. And, he had a two-two rifle and a box of bullets hidden in the outbuilding.

CHAPTER 3   THE FIRST WEEK IN FEBRUARY

The fact that the Assistant Chief Constable had turned up in Superintendent Blair's office in Skipton police station, with only an hour's notice, on a bright mild February morning, was not only a surprise to him but also of immediate concern. The ACC tended to be bad news for Blair, but, for once, he was wrong. The Chief Constable had given his second in command the latest news on the spending review for next year's budget. It had come down from the Minister himself and Skipton police were to be given an extra three hundred thousand pounds to pay for new recruitment and specialist training, and, frankly, for whatever Blair chose to spend it on. After much smiling and handshaking, and an explanation that made little sense, the ACC went on his way.

Blair knew why he had been given the money, just as he knew why DI Alan Tate was now Detective Chief Inspector. It was the nearest thing to an official bribe. Only six months ago, Peter Wilson, a retired Secret Service pen pusher, had lost his life in Scargill Cottage. After a full investigation by Skipton police, helped, if that's the right word, by MI5, all facts were known but no-one had been charged with any crime, much to the anguish of the Wilson family, and to the anger of both Blair and Tate. An inquest had been held in camera and, although newspaper reporters had suspected a cover up, nothing linking Jonathan Maxim or MI5 had appeared in the press. Highly unsatisfactory! But there was nothing that Blair could do about it, the Minister and the Secret Service had seen to that. Maxim had disappeared and his sister had returned to her life as the landlady of The Inn in Buckden, the wife of Tom Henshaw who, having been attacked by David Tanner, had, at least, received reasonable compensation. Yes, Blair and Tate were aware of so much and yet had been unable to affect anything that could be regarded as justice. From their point of view, the whole tragedy had been the fault of MI5 and, principally, of David Tanner.

That same morning, PC Mark Craven, who had worked alongside Tanner in the search for Maxim, visited The Inn to see how the Henshaws were getting on. This was partly down to curiosity and partly down to a feeling of guilt at what had happened to them, both of whom he regarded as innocents in the Wilson affair. Whether that was true of Sally was questionable but, as with most men, he was somewhat smitten by this beautiful woman. After chatting aimlessly to the couple for half an hour, he asked if they were going to sell Scargill Cottage, after all the horrors that had occurred there.

'No,' said Tom, 'there's someone living up there now.'

Sally glanced angrily at her husband.

'Oh, who?' asked Craven.

'My sister,' came the hurried reply from the pub landlady.

The young PC nodded and left to return to his duties, but as he drove back down to Skipton, he had a feeling of unease. He had been certain that the cottage would be sold. After all, three people had been killed there. He'd even thought about putting a bid in himself, if it was going cheap. And as for Sally's sister, after all his involvement in the investigation, he had no knowledge of her existence.

That lunchtime, as Craven entered the staff cafeteria to grab a sandwich, he was still brooding about Scargill Cottage. It didn't seem right! He searched out a familiar face and found it. He strode quickly over to a table on the far side of the room. Alan Tate looked up from the case file he was studying while he drank his coffee.

'And what can I do for you, Constable?' he said in mild irritation.

Craven detailed his visit to Buckden that morning.

'You see, sir, it doesn't make sense, does it? Surely, you would sell the place after everything that's happened. And, Mrs Henshaw's sister? Does she even have a sister?'

Tate looked puzzled. He knew full well that there was no sister. Yes, there was a brother, and a brother who had a penchant for women's clothing, but surely not!

'Thanks for the information, Constable. I will give it due consideration. From your point of view, ignore it for the moment. I'll get back to you if I need your input.'

Craven nodded and went to get his sandwich, slightly annoyed by his superior's attitude. After finishing his coffee, Tate went straight to Blair's office. He relayed the PC's information to his Superintendent.

'Well,' said Blair, 'it can't be Jonathan Maxim in Scargill Cottage. He must be safely locked away in an asylum somewhere by now. Odd though.'

'Yes, sir, it must be someone else, but who? Why would Sally Henshaw lie? She has no sister. I suppose it's none of our business.'

'None of our business, yes, but I'm curious. OK, Alan, see if you can find out who is up there. It's not official police business and let me stress that I don't want any policeman of mine visiting that place ever again, if it can be avoided.'

'I'll see what I can come up with, sir. Discreet enquiries.'

'Good. No hurry though,' said Blair. 'Remember, curiosity killed the cat.'

'Lucky I don't have a cat, sir.'

Tate left the office to return to his current case. Blair stared out of his window with an unjustifiable feeling of dread. He hated coincidences and his day seemed to be full of them, with the ACC turning up with what to him was a bribe emanating from the death of Peter Wilson at Scargill Cottage, and then Tate turning up to tell him that somebody was living there again. Should he just have ignored it? Too late now!

CHAPTER 4

Fred Denby was glancing at his phone, and then at his copy of the Racing Post, and then at the television, as he tried desperately to figure out the winner of the next race. Settling on Un De Sceaux, he placed a ten-pound bet online and focused on the race on the box while he sipped away at a bottle of beer.

'Bugger, second!' he shouted at the television as the race ended.

He put down the bottle, picked up his pen and started to make markings all over the race card for the following race. He was down fifty quid so far today.

There was a knock at his front door and in walked Jonathan Maxim, dressed to the nines in a stunning ladies' tweed outfit, as if he were a VIP visitor to Kelso.

'Thought I'd join you, Mister Denby, for an afternoon at the races,' he said in an affected posh voice. 'I have come to negate any losses you may be making today.'

Fred grinned.

'Looking good today, Jon my boy. Do I take it that you've brought me some cash?'

'Yes, Fred.'

He took a wodge of notes out of his jacket pocket and spread them out over the farmer's table.

'There's over two grand in twenties. Five hundred for the rifle as we agreed, and the rest for stuff I need. I've written it all down for you.'

Maxim handed a scrap of paper to the farmer. On it were precise details of the mobile phone and laptop that he required. Fred looked at it.

'I don't really know anything about this sort of thing, Jon,' he said. 'Anyway, haven't you got a phone and a computer at the cottage?'

'No phone, except the bugged land line, and no computer that's private, if you get my meaning. I need these, Fred, otherwise I won't have any money. I got the two grand off Sis, but it's a one off. I've written down the shop in Skipton where you can get them for me. Should cost fifteen hundred quid, or thereabouts. You can keep the rest.'

'What the hell's going on, Jon?' queried the farmer, looking genuinely concerned.

'I'm a prisoner, Fred,' came the reply. 'I work for the hush-hush people, but on their terms, otherwise they'll put me away for life. I can't go anywhere, either. They've even put a chip in me, GPS-ed, just like a spaniel. I'm surprised that I managed to come across to the farm without being stopped. It's awful, Fred.'

'That's a bloody disgrace!' retorted the farmer. ''I'll get the stuff for you, lad.'

Denby knew only some of what had gone on at Scargill Cottage months before. Peter Wilson had been found dead up on Mastiles Lane, miles away, and Mrs Elaine Law, Jonathan's mother, had died under suspicious circumstances at the cottage, but the press hadn't managed to link the two deaths. Newspaper reports had gone quiet and locals were left with half-truths and innuendo. The farmer had helped Jonathan many times over the years. He had been very well rewarded, especially when he'd aided Jonathan and his sister's flight from Wharfedale. He wasn't about to look this gift horse in the mouth. The bottom line was that, as ever, he needed money for the horses.

Three days later, Jonathan Maxim had the new phone and laptop. He could tether the laptop to the phone and have access to the web through a standard network provider, totally unknown to GCHQ or MI5. He was back in business! All this could have been done through Sally but that would have put her at risk. For the time being, he would do as his masters demanded, but he intended getting his money back. They had emptied his accounts and one point seven million dollars was a lot to lose! He hadn't stolen the money, after all. Well, not in his own mind at any rate.

As the days passed by, Jonathan became more and more resentful of his plight and the restrictions on his movement. The worst thing was the GPS chip, being treated like a dog. If ever he needed to get away, he'd have to dig that chip out of his own shoulder with a knife!

One afternoon, David Tanner burst into Scargill Cottage, unannounced. With Maxim standing bolt upright in the middle of his room, hands clasped together in anger, the MI5 man searched through the whole building. He found nothing. The phone and the laptop were well hidden behind a removable wooden wall panel in Maxim's mother's bedroom.

'Just checking,' said Tanner, not knowing what he was checking for. 'I know you've been over to see Fred Denby, more than once. I wouldn't trust that farmer with a barge pole.'

'An unusual object for a Dales farmer, don't you think, Mister Tanner?' said Maxim with an effeminate smile. 'Yes, I've seen Fred a few times, for a drink and a chat. You wouldn't want me to go mad in this place, would you, on my own, with no-one to talk to? You're hardly a conversationalist!'

'You're only supposed to see your sister,' said Tanner, firmly, 'but, so long as you don't get up to mischief, Denby can be your soulmate.'

'Fred suggested that we might go to Catterick races next week. I would wear my tweed outfit. It's very smart. You could follow me on GPS!'

'No chance!' shouted Tanner as he slammed the front door behind him.

As he drove back down to Kettlewell he too felt angry. From day to day he monitored Maxim, he read his emails and he did bugger all else, except for the odd visit to a local pub and one too many whiskies. He only visited the cottage a couple of times a week and invariably came away feeling that he'd just lost another verbal joust. As it was for Maxim, it would be another six months or so before Tanner's own situation would be reviewed. He was bored, and he was playing nursemaid to a dangerous schizophrenic. 'If only something would happen,' he often said to himself. Then again, maybe boredom wasn't too bad!

CHAPTER 5

It had been a simple instruction to PC Craven from DCI Tate.

'Go up to Buckden. See Mrs Henshaw and tell her she doesn't have a sister. Then ask her who's really living in Scargill Cottage. And be nice about it.'

So, on a clear bright morning, around half past ten, Mark Craven knocked on the main entrance door to The Inn. No-one answered. He walked round the back of the small whitewashed pub. The car park was empty which, from memory, probably meant that both Henshaws were out. Craven was annoyed with himself. He should have rung the pub before he set off.

'Maybe Mrs Henshaw has gone to the cottage,' he thought and, even though Tate had told him not to go up there, he decided he would.

He continued up the dale and turned left at Cray, up a winding road for a mile or so, before turning right to enter the driveway between conifers, some two hundred yards from Scargill Cottage. As the marked police car moved slowly along the tarmac, Jonathan Maxim watched via the surveillance camera screen before moving quickly around his room, altering his appearance as he went. He meticulously added a bobbed fair-haired wig to his attire, a red chunky knitted sweater and dark knee-length skirt, complete with black tights and smart flat shoes. As the uniformed officer approached the cottage along the narrow garden path, Jonathan opened the front door in welcome. He recognised Craven from months before when he had come to the cottage with David Tanner to ask his mother questions.

'Hello officer,' he said in a quiet voice. 'Is there something wrong? I've never had a visit from the police before.'

Sally Henshaw had forewarned her brother that the police might show up. Mark Craven stared at the person in front of him. She was slim, slight and rather attractive. He smiled.

'Oh, nothing wrong, madam, just part of my rounds, you might say. I'm calling to see if everything is OK. No trouble with walkers or nosey parkers? After recent events we just wanted to check that you were having no problems. In fact, we were unaware that anyone was living up here now. Sorry to ask, but may I have your name?'

The response was an outrageous smile.

'I'm Jenny Henshaw,' came the reply. 'You may know my brother and sister-in-law at the public house in Buckden. I moved in at the start of January. Rent free of course. I'm just staying here for a few months while my new flat in Leeds is being done up. Would you like to come in officer?

For a cup of tea and a biscuit? I rarely have anyone to chat to.'

Craven quickly digested the mistake that he thought he'd made. This was Mrs Henshaw's sister-in-law, not her sister. He said 'yes' to the offer and followed Jonathan into the front room, noticeably chastising himself with a shake of the head. For the next twenty minutes he made pleasant conversation between sips of tea, before enquiring as to whether Fred Denby had visited from the next-door farm.

'Oh yes, such a nice man,' the officer was told. 'He kept an eye on the cottage for Sally and Tom after the, erm, anyway, he's been most helpful. I have seen him a couple of times. Well, officer, I mustn't keep you from your duties, and I do have a few things I must do.'

Craven immediately stood and thanked his host for his cup of tea.

He left the cottage fully convinced that he had met and enjoyed the company of Miss Jenny Henshaw. He'd been quite taken with his hostess and drove back down through Cray in a very good mood. As he reached Buckden and passed The Inn, Tom Henshaw was in the rear car park, busy unloading his Landrover with stock for the bar, while Sally was answering a phone call from her brother in her bedroom. She was laughing very loudly.

'Jonny, you're outrageous,' she said. 'But we can't have this happening again. This is MI5's fault. I'll find David

Tanner in Kettlewell and tell him to tell the police to leave you alone. That poor policeman is going to feel very stupid!'

An hour later, with the help of an estate agent in the centre of Kettlewell, Sally had ascertained Tanner's location. She knocked vigorously on the door of a small terraced cottage just off the main street. A somewhat shocked David Tanner opened the door to receive a tirade of verbal abuse. It ended with:

'So, if you want my brother to get on with his work for you lot, and not stress out, I suggest you tell the police to stay away!'

The golden-haired vision then turned on a sixpence and stormed off.

Late that afternoon, DCI Tate was summoned to Superintendent Blair's office in Skipton police station. As he entered the room, he glanced left to see David Tanner, someone he particularly disliked, sitting a few feet away from Blair's desk. Tanner nodded. Tate did not.

'Would you care to enlighten the DCI as to who is living in Scargill Cottage and what the overall situation is, Mister Tanner?'

Tanner gave Tate fifteen minutes of enlightenment, interrupted several times by expletives and expressions of disbelief.

'So, the bottom line is that a dangerous killer is back up there, working for the Secret Service on God knows what, and must be left alone!' shouted Tate at both Tanner and his superior.

'Yes, Alan,' said Blair in a quiet but firm voice. 'Remember, even after all that happened a few months ago, no formal charges could be brought against Jonathan Maxim, and it turns out that he is a very valuable asset.'

'Yes, sir, but he could be a very valuable asset somewhere else, surely, rather than on our patch!'

Tate knew he was overstepping the mark. He turned, left the office, and slammed the door behind him.

Blair sighed and then turned to Tanner.

'I shall be writing to the Chief Constable about this matter, Mister Tanner.'

'It'll do you no favours, Superintendent. This has all been sanctioned by the Minister. Maxim will probably only be here for six months. And then, who knows? Yes, he can be unstable, but he remains under permanent medication and has been tagged. I'm here to make sure nothing goes awry. And his sister is crucial to his well-being. Without her, we'd never get anything out of him. That's why he's got to be on your patch, if only for a while.'

Blair nodded and added, with finality:

'Make sure nothing does go awry, Mister Tanner. For the time being, goodbye.'

David Tanner hurriedly left and brushed past DCI Tate in the corridor outside. Tate went back into Blair's office and apologised to his boss. The two men chatted for over half an hour, both exceedingly worried about Jonathan Maxim's return to Wharfedale.

CHAPTER 6

During his first six weeks tied digitally to GCHQ, Jonathan Maxim was perceived to be fulfilling his part of the bargain rather well, but a bargain that, in his own head, he had never made. He acted daily as a mentor to cyber specialists, showing them many of the tricks that he had taught himself over the years, but he had also been given the task of hunting down hackers. This was proving to be his greatest worth to GCHQ. He was able to identify four gold-star hackers, all based in eastern Europe, who had severely disrupted American and UK defence sites during the previous year. Their true names and locations were now known to MI6. Maxim assumed that they would be dealt with very quickly. He had no conscience about such matters. Underneath it all, he believed himself to be some sort of patriot. His father had worked covertly within the SAS for MI5 and MI6, and he too had assisted in such activities within the UK and Ireland during his early twenties. He still felt some pang of regret about the Garda officer but, what the hell, he shouldn't have got in the way.

GCHQ believed that they knew everything that Maxim had found out about the four hackers, but that was not quite correct. Jonathan had purposefully withheld vital information. He had discovered what linked them all, and that link was money. These were not disruptive teenagers, they were professionals working as a team and were very highly paid, over a million dollars in total. What is more, he'd found out where the money came from. Through their own websites, sites that he had hacked invisibly, he had traced four separate Swiss bank accounts that their ill-gotten gains had been paid into. It had taken him days of painstaking work but, from those accounts, he had been able to follow the money trail back through linked websites around the world, to a unique source. That source was a bank account in his beloved Douglas, on the Isle of Man, and that account was held in the name of Yevgeni Galerkin. Finding out all about Galerkin had been trivially easy. Google! This Russian was a respectable billionaire oligarch living in London, well known for mixing with the higher echelons of society and bankrolling a London football club.

Jonathan Maxim was not interested in Galerkin per se, but he was extremely interested in his money. He resented the emptying of his accounts by the British Secret Service. MI5 would never give him back the one point seven million dollars they'd stolen from him, but Galerkin could. That sum of money was chicken feed to an oligarch. His account in Douglas held eighty-nine million dollars.

For over a week, Jonathan largely abandoned his GCHQ hardware in favour of his modest laptop and phone, courtesy of Fred Denby. He knew that he was taking a risk. The phone provider's security was poor in comparison, but the game was worth it. His need for excitement, and for the thrill of winning, spurred him on. He wouldn't just take one point seven million, he'd take the lot! For days he worked on the software he needed and studied the Chamberland Asset Bank security systems and protocols in detail. By the end of the month everything was in place. At midnight on the last day in February, Galerkin's Isle of Man account simply disappeared. Ironically, his eighty-nine million dollars were transferred to a newly created account in another bank in Douglas only a quarter of a mile away, a bank previously used by Maxim and his sister to hide funds. At the very instant that Jonathan Maxim pressed the enter key on his laptop to make the transfer, he shouted out the word *nostrovia* and went through to the kitchen to make himself a cup of tea, laughing all the way.

It was two days later, when Yevgeni Galerkin attempted to withdraw a considerable amount of money from a now non-existent account, that Chamberland Asset Bank realised that something was drastically wrong and that their security had been compromised. All accounts were immediately frozen. Within an hour, two senior executives were on a flight to London for a very embarrassing interview with one of their most valuable clients. Both sides had plenty of paperwork to prove the existence of the account and the monies involved and Galerkin was assured that his losses would be made good and that CAB's security had been strengthened and made impenetrable with immediate effect. This would not and could not happen again. Since the bank clearly had no idea of who had committed the theft, or how they had managed to accomplish it, the oligarch did not believe them. He knew that he was now vulnerable and that he had been deliberately targeted. But by whom?

The following day Galerkin was given the news that three of his most valued employees, two in Bulgaria and the other in Slovakia, were dead. Provisionally, the official causes of death were suicide, a car accident and a fall from a balcony. When, on the same day, a fourth's apartment in Bucharest was entered by a British agent, the bird had flown. That bird, a Russian named Anton Davidov, was safely back in Moscow visiting his sick mother. He received a long rambling angry email from his master that ended with a single curt instruction.

'Find the man who stole my money!'

CHAPTER 7   MARCH THE FIRST

It was March the first, a sunny almost Spring-like day. Jonathan Maxim woke early and said 'white rabbits' to himself, something he'd copied from his father for good luck since the age of five. He showered in the corner of his room before dressing in jeans and blouse and blow drying his hair. He took his pills as per instruction and was ready for his day.

His morning was spent at his official workstation, answering further GCHQ questions about the team of hackers. What had been their future targets? How well coordinated were they? And who was running them? He gave very fulsome answers to the first two questions and lied about the last, with 'I don't know yet. Will investigate.' He had decided not to mention Galerkin, a powerful man with a long reach, someone who may have infiltrated the British establishment itself. Better to keep quiet, having pocketed eighty-nine million dollars of oligarch funds! By lunchtime he had tired of GCHQ. He switched off the workstation and moved to his own laptop.

All afternoon he played chess online. He was a paying member of a rather select chess club consisting of one hundred fellow enthusiasts, run by two Grand Masters. He himself was ninth on the chess ladder. His aim was to be ranked in the top three. That afternoon he played an

American ranked sixth and won. He was ecstatic. Not only did he rise in the rankings, but he also won a prize. Fifty dollars!

At five o'clock Sally and Tom arrived. It was most unusual for his brother-in-law to visit him. Jonathan had only ever met Tom Henshaw a few times before, the last time being in the first few days after his return to Scargill Cottage in January. He couldn't remember ever having a meaningful conversation with him. Sally went through to the kitchen to put away provisions that she'd brought, and to make a hot meal, while Tom sat himself down in the lounge opposite Jonathan. He clearly wanted to talk.

'Sally's been telling me about your situation here, Jonathan. Not good, but we feel very strongly that you should do as they want for the six months and then, hopefully, you'll have your life back.'

'Oh dear,' thought Jonathan, 'my brother-in-law, hardly the brightest bunny in the hutch, is here to give me a pep talk. Sal must be worried.'

He assured Tom that he was taking his medication, that he was feeling happy and positive, that he was doing exactly what his masters demanded, and that he would not jeopardise either his own future or the future of his beloved sister. Tom smiled effusively. Sally had listened from the kitchen and shook her head. She knew her brother far too well and was less convinced. After eating curry, Jonathan and his sister did the washing up while Tom walked around the small front garden asking himself what more he could do to help. He should play a bigger role in his brother-in-law's life.

'I had a quick look in your room, Jonny,' Sally said to her brother. 'You have a shiny new laptop and a very upmarket smartphone. Fred Denby, I assume. Tanner would be very displeased. Are you're getting up to mischief?'

Jonathan sniggered.

'Just a little fun, Sis. No need to worry. I can play my chess and do bits of things in private, that's all.'

'You're not playing the stock markets again, are you? They took the million dollars back, Jonny. They'd do it again if necessary. And you're not playing with the bank in Dougie, are you?'

Dougie was what the brother and sister called Douglas on the Isle of Man, remembering their seaside holidays there as children.

'I wouldn't risk doing anything like that, Sal.'

'Mmm, so what's the real reason for having the bloody laptop, Jonny!' she shouted at him.

Jonathan immediately began to sulk. He could not cope with being told off by his sister.

'I shall ask you again,' she said. 'And next time you'd better have a convincing answer.'

She shouted to Tom that it was time to go and the two of them drove back down to Buckden, leaving Jonathan to mull things over.

For two hours he lay on his bed, wondering whether to tell Sally what he'd been up to. No, he wouldn't, but he mustn't take too many risks!

It was at about nine-thirty when the silence in the cottage was broken by a single pistol shot echoing in the darkness outside. Maxim pinpointed it as coming from some way down the tarmac drive. He leapt from the bed, raced to the back door and within thirty seconds was in the outbuilding with the loaded two-two rifle in his hands. He skirted the rear of the cottage, ran to his right and, keeping to the edge of the wood, moved at rapid speed towards the conifer screen at the end of the drive. As he got within fifty yards of the conifers, he heard a car screaming away down the winding hillside to Cray. He stopped and listened intently. There was no sound. He walked forward slowly and then stood stock still on the tarmac between the conifers, rifle readied, studying, as best he could, the wooded area to the left and right of him.

'Why the hell fire a shot and then run away?' he thought.

His eyes fixed on something in the ragged grass nearby, lit by moonlight. He walked cautiously towards it. It was the body of a man lying on his back, legs together but arms spread out, like a horizontal crucifixion. Sticking out from his chest was a thin broken knife blade. Maxim reached down to examine the blade but then pulled his hand away.

'Stupid, Jonny,' he said to himself. 'Mustn't leave any fingerprints or DNA.'

He bent down and stared into the dead eyes staring back up at him.

'Well, I've no idea who you are, but someone didn't like you very much.'

He jogged back to the cottage for a torch and then returned. He didn't touch the body or the man's clothing. That would have been too risky. He searched around the area systematically and found, a few feet from the body, a revolver. He checked it to find that it had been fired only once, with five bullets remaining. Close by his torch alighted on the reflection of something lying at the foot of a tree. He realised that it was a photograph. He picked it up and turned it over to reveal the image. His reaction was at first curiosity followed by sudden anger. He stiffened his right arm and pointed the revolver at the dead man's head but, when just about to pull the trigger, he raised the gun to the dark sky and fired five shots, screaming to the heavens as he did so.

He took time to calm himself. None of this made sense, but he must take care. He had nothing to do with this killing, but would anyone believe him? He returned to the outbuilding and hid the two-two. Back in the cottage he secreted the revolver and the photograph, along with the laptop and phone, behind the wooden panel in his mother's room. He then showered and dressed in different clothes.

He went through to the front room and paced around for minutes on end, thinking. He had no good options. He thought that he was being set up by someone, but why, and by whom? MI5 had no reason to do this. They could have put him away months ago, for good. He would have to trust Tanner. He rang his sister on the landline phone, not seeing what his security cameras were seeing in his den. He explained very calmly and carefully what had happened, except that he missed out the revolver and the photograph. He was back in control now.

'Phone Tanner,' he instructed her. 'You've got his number? He must sort this out. MI5 can get rid of the body. I'm being set up, Sal.'

'Will do, Jonny. Take care,' she replied, immediately phoning the number Tanner had belatedly given her.

Maxim had just put down the phone when four armed policemen burst through the front door. Within seconds he was on the floor, hands cuffed behind his back, being shouted at incoherently. As he was dragged to his feet, he stared at the open doorway. In walked a face that he had never seen. It was DCI Alan Tate.

Most of Tate's day had been mundane. His morning was spent checking paperwork put together by his Detective Sergeant. Trueman believed that they had enough evidence now to arrest the gang suspected of sheep rustling. Over a hundred sheep had gone missing from three farms near Starbotton. He had lunch with Trueman and gave him the go ahead. In the afternoon he had a long meeting with Superintendent Blair about targets. He hated pedantic admin. At six o'clock he went home and had a blazing row with his wife Anne about something trivial as he ate a substandard takeaway pizza, washed down with a glass of beer. He felt guilty about the argument and apologised. It didn't help. He settled himself in front of the television to watch one of his wife's favourite films, a film he particularly disliked. He was trying to make amends. He soon fell asleep in his chair.

Just before ten his house phone rang. Anne answered it.

'Phone. For you Alan! It's work!' she shouted. Tate got slowly out of his chair and trudged across to his wife. She thrust the phone into his right hand.

'Hello, DCI Tate speaking,' he said.

It was DS Trueman.

'Sir, we've just had a 999 call from a Mister Merriweather. He lives in Cray. He said he was out walking his dog and heard several shots coming from Scargill Cottage, near the entrance to the drive, he thought. He saw car lights come down the hill fast but had no more information.'

Tate might have been suspicious of the call but all the events of last summer came flooding back. In his mind there was a dangerous schizophrenic up there. Better to act quickly with force and look foolish, than wait until the morning to investigate! Tate rang Superintendent Blair. This time, Skipton police were up to speed. Within twenty-five minutes an armed assault team, followed in a marked police car by Tate, Trueman and PC Craven, the only one of them who had ever met Jonathan Maxim, were hurtling up the dale.

At ten-fifty a sharp-eyed officer spotted the dead body lying within the conifer screen that marked the entrance to Scargill Cottage driveway. Tate gave the order to move in and move in fast!

When he walked into the cottage the handcuffed man before him looked nothing like what he had imagined. The killer of Peter Wilson, or so he was in Tate's view, was a handsome effeminate twenty-eight-year-old who smiled engagingly at Craven as he entered behind the DCI.

'We meet again, officer,' said Maxim, feigning a kiss, seemingly unfazed by events. Craven flushed with embarrassment.

Trueman threw Maxim backwards into a chair and had to be restrained by his superior.

While Tate and Craven stood over Maxim, neither man speaking, the rest of the police team began searching the cottage and the outbuilding. They were thorough but found nothing. When, finally, Trueman returned, Tate ordered:

'OK, get him out of here.'

At that moment, in walked Superintendent Blair accompanied by David Tanner and Sally Henshaw.

'Hi Sal. Glad you made it. And you, MI5.'

Maxim irritated the hell out of Tanner.

'I'm arresting Jonathan Maxim on suspicion of murder, sir,' said Tate to his superior, unnerved somewhat by Blair's arrival. Blair sighed.

'No, you're not, Detective Chief Inspector, at least not yet. We are handing custody of Mister Maxim over to Mister Tanner. The Secret Service are taking responsibility for him. He will be confined here with Mister Tanner until matters are resolved.'

Maxim stared at Tanner who stared back.

'Don't worry Jonny, I'll be here too,' said Sally calmly to her brother.

'Let's get the crime scene sorted,' said Blair to Tate. 'Doctor Jones should be here soon with his team. We need all the forensics we can get on this one. Then we'll see about an arrest.'

He turned to Tanner and whispered, 'Don't bugger this up.'

'Mrs Henshaw,' he added as he nodded at Sally and walked out of the front door followed by the police team, the last of which handed the keys to the handcuffs to Tanner, with a smile.

An hour later Tom Henshaw arrived with two suitcases. There would be four of them in Scargill Cottage that night.

Tom was met by his wife at the door. She took him through to mother's bedroom to calm him down and talk things over. He had wanted to be more a part of Jonathan's life but...

David Tanner interrogated Jonathan for over two hours, going over and over his story. Maxim's replies were comprehensive, calm and completely consistent with each other. In the end he started to believe him, even though he didn't want to. Maxim, still handcuffed, was locked in his room for the night. Tanner would sleep on the sofa in the front room. At three o'clock in the morning his phone rang.

'What the hell is going on, David?' asked Dawson. 'I've just had a tirade from the Minister.'

'Well, sir,' said Tanner, 'someone has indeed ended up dead and I've got no idea who it is, who did it, or why. Goodnight sir.'

He switched off his phone.

CHAPTER 8

By just after one-thirty the forensic team had completed its initial investigation of the crime scene and the examination of the body, led by chief pathologist Doctor Eric Jones. The body was transported back to his main lab in Leeds ready for a full autopsy in the morning. The night's darkness was lit by blinding arc lights and the whole of the surrounding area was thoroughly searched by police. There were plenty of footprints to photograph but nothing truly useful was discovered. The dead man was wearing a smart suit, and smart shoes. Clearly this was no local walker out for an evening stroll in the countryside! Sure enough, fifty yards up the road, parked askew on the bumpy grass verge, was a car. Behind it was a mess of skidding tyre tracks. Another vehicle had obviously been there but had turned around and left in a hurry.

Tate ended the night's work at two o'clock, ready for an early start in the morning.

The police invaded the hamlet of Cray shortly after eight, with Tate, Craven and PC Helen Warren, who had shown herself to be very capable when helping with the Wilson case, doing a house to house of the six houses and one pub,

The Lion. Tate and Warren, with a ready smile and relaxed manner, would deal with the residents. Mister Merriweather was the first to be interviewed but gave no more information than that gleaned from his phone call the previous evening. He had heard shots, but he wasn't sure how many, and had seen headlights moving at great speed down the hill towards the village. He may have heard shouting but wasn't sure and the order in which things had happened were blurred. Strangely, none of the other residents remembered a car, or car headlights, coming down through the village after nine. There had been a car quite a bit earlier, but that was Fred Denby in his Rover, going for a few pints, something he did on a very regular basis. Drink driving never concerned Fred on a mile and a half climb back up to Scargill Farm.

The Lion was situated two miles from Buckden, on a winding stretch of the main road as it climbed over to Wensleydale. It stood a hundred yards or so from the few houses on the side road that constituted Cray. It had no car park to speak of, just a pull in on the other side of the road, big enough for half a dozen cars or so. As Mark Craven approached the pub, a pub he had been in a few times himself, he saw the old Rover. He walked straight in. The young landlord, who had taken on the pub five years before, was busy providing hearty breakfasts for two couples from London who were having a walking break in Wharfedale. In a dimly lit corner of the bar, seemingly fast asleep and snoring quietly, sounding more like a dozing terrier than a sixty-year-old Yorkshire farmer, was Fred Denby. Craven left him in peace. He walked through to the breakfasting area. As the young walkers ate, he sat with the landlord, quietly asking him what he knew of the night before.

'So, Terry, was it busy in here last night? From six onwards, say.'

'No, officer. The walkers,' replied the landlord, nodding across to their table, 'they arrived about half past eight. I settled them in their rooms and then made them some food, fish and chips all round.'

'And the bar?'

'There were two lads who'd come down from Buckden Pike. They had a pint and a sandwich about seven. Said they were staying in Starbotton, camping. Left soon after.'

'And Mister Denby? How come he's fast asleep in the bar?'

'Well,' continued Terry, 'for once, even Fred couldn't make it back up to Scargill Farm in that Rover of his. He couldn't find his keys and, to be frank, he was as drunk as a skunk. He started drinking before eight and stopped at about eleven when I told him to. He must have had five pints and three or four whiskies by then. He nodded off. The walkers had already retired for the night, so I switched the lights off and went to bed.'

'You saw no-one else?'

'No,' said the landlord, before adding, 'except the American.'

Craven stared back open-mouthed.

'American, what American?'

'Oh, sorry, yes, the American, well he sounded American to me. He came in about the same time as these four, or maybe just before. He asked about the Triangle Walk and how to get to Scargill Cottage. He seemed nice enough. He stood at the bar with a glass of coke. I didn't see him leave.'

'Did he talk to Mr Denby?'

'Not sure. Maybe, maybe not. Fred was on his third pint by then, at least.'

Craven thanked the landlord and let him get on with his work. He walked through to the bar. Fred was gone. Walking outside, so was the Rover.

'Damn,' exclaimed Tate as Craven came to the end of his news. 'Well, you'll have to interview Denby, the American might have said something to him. Well done, Craven. So, the dead man is an American.'

'Or the killer,' said Craven.

'I don't think so,' replied Tate. 'I examined the man's shoes and suit. Italian shoes, but the suit was made in good old New York.' He smiled.

Tate, Craven and Warren left Cray and headed up to the crime scene where DS Trueman and his team had just finished their second search and had tidied up. Trueman handed car keys taken from the dead man's jacket pocket to PC Warren.

'Get that car back to Skipton for further forensics, Helen,' he said, pointing across at the vehicle.

Soon, the area around the conifers was back to its usual state. Two hundred yards away Jonathan Maxim had watched the proceedings on screen as best he could, via the security cameras, while David Tanner observed from the front room using a small pair of binoculars. Tom and Sally had walked outside into the garden but quickly returned to their bedroom when waved at by an armed policeman halfway down the drive. By midday, all the police had gone, except for two officers with automatic weapons who stood guard at the end of the driveway. No-one was coming in and no-one was going out!

Tanner rang Superintendent Blair and became angry.

'No, Mister Tanner, you must stay put until I've met with DCI Tate and the chief pathologist later today. I will get back to you this evening if possible. And before you ask, all this has been OK-ed by my boss and your boss.'

Tanner swore and ended the call.

Five minutes later his phone sprang into life with an inconsequential ring tone that he'd become sick of months ago. It was DCI Tate who spent thirty minutes going through the details of Maxim's account of the previous night.

'So, you're telling me that Maxim says that he ran towards where he'd heard several shots coming from, carrying no weapon to defend himself with, not even a kitchen knife. Is that plausible?'

Tanner did not take well to being interrogated.

'Look Tate,' he said defiantly, 'that's what he told me. He is perfectly capable of killing someone without a knife. He was trained by his father. The guy was SAS!'

'So, do you think he killed the American?'

'Jesus, American!' exclaimed Tanner. 'How do you know he was American? What the hell is going on here? I believe that Maxim did not kill anyone last night, but I cannot be sure. He is always so convincing.'

The call ended soon after with frustration on both sides.

CHAPTER 9

Everyone was summoned to be in Blair's office at precisely five o'clock that afternoon. To the Superintendent's surprise, Doctor Jones knocked and entered ten minutes early, most unusual for the ever-busy pathologist. He tossed his report down onto a small table and sat down next to it, folding his arms with a knowing smile, something Blair was used to. As the clock on the wall ticked past five, there was a knock on the door and Tate, Trueman and Craven entered the room. All three sat facing Blair, with Jones some way to the side.

'Let us start with the pathologist's report, eh, Doctor Jones. What can you tell us?'

Jones consulted his report, although he had no need to.

'The dead man was about fifty-five years of age, probably American, judging by his dental work, but he had no identification about his person. He had a broken knife blade protruding from his chest, having penetrated his right lung and resulting in much internal bleeding, but this did not kill him. I believe that a sharp single blow to his right temple was the cause of death. Out like a light, permanently. The technical detail is in the report.'

'So,' asked Blair, 'the blow could have come from an expert, or from an amateur who got lucky?'

'Precisely. Such a technique would be well known to someone trained to kill, but, then again, I have come across such a death as a result of a minor teenage fracas,' replied Jones.

'What about the blade?' asked Tate. 'A professional's weapon or a kitchen knife or what?'

Jones smiled.

'No forensics to speak of but, well, the blade is rather curious,' he said. 'It takes me back to the days of my youth. A colleague of mine came up with this one. The broken blade, which is not very substantial, appears to be from a flick knife, circa 1950s or 60s, not something you would expect to be carried by your average professional killer methinks.'

'So,' said Blair once again, sighing somewhat, 'it could be a hitman pretending to be an amateur, but why?'

'Your territory, not mine, Superintendent,' replied Jones. 'Now, gentlemen, I must get on. More bodies back in Leeds, I'm afraid. Please get back to me with any further questions.'

With that he nodded at Blair and left the room.

'Mmm,' said Tate, 'I don't think that helps us a lot, except that I don't really see Maxim carrying a flick knife or currently having access to one. A knife is his weapon of choice though, according to Tanner, and he is SAS trained.'

'Yes, yes,' said Blair in annoyance. 'OK Alan, what have you three got for me?'

Tate started by telling his superior what Maxim had told Tanner. He had heard five or six shots, dashed outside, heard a car leave at speed, found the body and returned to the cottage, where he rang his sister before police arrived.

'Do you believe his story?' asked Blair.

'If it's true, sir, then it's a hell of a coincidence that a man is killed by a single blow but not by the one man definitely capable of doing it who lives in a cottage only two hundred yards away.'

'Point taken, Alan. What do we know about the victim?'

'We now know who he is. His passport, credit cards, etcetera, were hidden in the car we brought back to Skipton. Very well hidden, sir. We have also been in touch with the American embassy. They confirmed that the man was John Donnelly, a resident of New York, aged 57, a retired US Government employee.'

'What sort of employee?'

'The US embassy said that they couldn't tell us, sir.'

'Couldn't or wouldn't?' asked Blair rhetorically. 'Perhaps Mister Tanner, or that boss of his, might be able to find out for us. Did you find anything out in Cray?'

'Not much, sir. Mister Merriweather, who made the 999 call, had no more to offer. Oddly, no residents heard or saw a car speeding down through the village around nine-thirty. PC Craven made enquiries at The Lion pub. Craven.'

Mark Craven told Blair about his conversation with the landlord and about Fred Denby's presence in, and then disappearance from, the pub.'

'So, have you caught up with the errant farmer?' asked Blair.'

'Yes, sir, earlier this afternoon. I spotted his green Rover in Kettlewell. All he said was that he'd had a bit too much to drink, an understatement according to the landlord, and had fallen asleep, only to wake in the morning to find a policeman, me sir, in the pub, so he'd legged it. However, he did say that he had seen an American in the bar. He'd come over to him and asked if he knew who lived up at Scargill Cottage. Denby said that he told him no-one lived there. It was what Mrs Henshaw had wanted, no intruders. Apparently, the man just smiled and then left the pub.'

'Have you anything to add, DS Trueman? What's the state of play up at the cottage?'

'Four in the cottage, sir, with Maxim locked in his room and Tanner getting a bit twitchy. I stationed two armed officers at the end of the drive. The crime scene's spick and span now. We know that there was another car up there, not just the American's. It left in a hurry by the look of the tyre tracks, just as Maxim said, but we can't make anything of them. Too muddy, sir.'

'Thank you, Detective Sergeant. Right Alan, what do we think?' Blair said, hoping for agreement.

'I think we arrest Maxim. We need to question him ourselves and he's the only suspect we have. And we need to search the cottage thoroughly, and the surroundings. There might be weapons or forensics that we don't know about yet. Tanner won't be happy, but he never is.'

'Agreed, Alan. I will inform Tanner myself. You go up there, now, and arrest Maxim. Bring him and Tanner back here and make sure the Henshaws return to Buckden. We then seal off Scargill Cottage and go through it with a fine-toothed comb.'

'Right, gentlemen, get on with it,' he added.

Blair watched the ever-present jackdaws from his window for fifteen minutes before having the expected heated conversation with David Tanner.

By seven o'clock, an angry and increasingly unstable Jonathan Maxim was in a cell in Skipton police station, awaiting interrogation the following morning, without the support of his sister who was back home with her husband, terrified about the effect this would have on her brother. David Tanner had refused to accompany Maxim to Skipton and was in Kettlewell, on his phone to Dawson explaining what had happened and demanding help.

Up at Scargill Cottage, the police team led by Trueman searched everywhere. They found the two-two rifle in the outbuilding but not Jonathan Maxim's laptop or phone, or the revolver, or the photograph. They left his workstation well alone.

'That's the property of GCHQ,' had been Maxim's taunt when he left the cottage in handcuffs.

CHAPTER 10

At nine forty-five the following morning David Tanner was in Superintendent Blair's office, accompanied by Sally Henshaw. Blair had agreed to Tanner being present when Jonathan Maxim was interviewed, after discussing it with DCI Tate over the phone, just an hour before. Tanner had a further request.

'Mrs Henshaw asks to be present at the interview, Superintendent, and wishes to provide Jonathan with legal representation. She has also brought his medication which is vital to his wellbeing.'

'Medication, fine,' interrupted Tate, 'but legal representation, I doubt that.'

Tate smiled at Blair. Sally looked daggers at them both.

'I do have a first-class degree in Law from UCL and the requisite solicitor training.'

She stared coldly at the DCI.

'You needn't look so shocked Mister Tate. I may not be quite as pretty as my brother, but he's not the only one with brains in the family!'

Tanner stifled a laugh. Tate was no verbal match for this stunning adversary. As he opened his mouth to reply, Blair held up his right hand to calm proceedings and agreed to Sally's demand.

At ten o'clock Jonathan Maxim, in handcuffs, entered the box-like interview room and took the seat next to his sister, opposite Tate and Trueman, the latter switching on the recording equipment and saying a few words. Tanner sat some way off in a corner of the room. Sally held a glass of water to her brother's mouth and he swallowed two tablets which had an immediate calming effect.

The first forty minutes went by just as Jonathan expected, with his story of events being picked apart by Tate, but to little effect.

'To reiterate, you dashed from the cottage unarmed, ran towards where you heard shots coming from, and discovered the dead man. You had heard three pistol shots. That's what you claim?'

'Yes, but more like five or six shots, for the tenth time,' replied Maxim.

'You didn't take your two-two rifle with you?'

Maxim looked concerned, as did Tanner. Sally fixed an angry stare on her brother's face.

'Oh, yes,' said Tate triumphantly, 'we found the rifle and a partially full box of bullets, hidden, but not well enough, in the outbuilding. Clearly, you have not mentioned this to your legal representative or your minder. You see, Jonathan, it's like this. We know from your GPS chip info, provided by Mister Tanner, that your movements were pretty much as you describe, and we know from a local dog walker that several shots were fired, but we don't know that they were pistol shots. It's only you who say that they were. What I think is that you fired shots at the man, that you missed, and that you then stabbed him. You're the killer here. Am I right, Jonathan?'

Jonathan thought hard before answering.

'OK, yes I took the rifle with me, but I never used it. The man was dead. Anyway, what about the knife blade, and what about the car I heard tear away? Did your dog walker confirm that? He must have heard it.'

Tate continued.

'You could have thrown the knife handle away at any time later. As for the car, yes, there was another car, but that could have been the dead man's accomplice who you might have wounded with the rifle. That would explain the shots and a hurried escape.'

'You're an idiot!' shouted Maxim. 'Ask Tanner who I am and what my father was. He taught me. I don't use knives with handles that snap off, and I could shoot you between the eyes from two hundred metres or more, even with Fred's popgun!'

'Ah, so that's where you got the gun. Stolen from the farmer. Perhaps Mister Tanner should monitor your GPS more closely.'

Tanner considered joining in but thought better of it. This wasn't going well for him, let alone Maxim. Sally Henshaw interjected.

'DCI Tate. Tell me, do you have any forensic evidence directly linking my brother to this killing? He has clearly behaved as might be expected, when hearing shots. Essentially, he has been confined to Scargill Cottage for weeks now, to work for UK authorities, and has been placed in a vulnerable position. His contention is that either someone was there to kill him, or, perhaps more probably, to frame him for the murder of a man about which he knows nothing.'

Jonathan was pleased with his sister's intervention.

'I did look closely at the man's face. I've never seen him before.'

'Does the name John Donnelly mean anything to you?' asked Tate.

Maxim took a sharp intake of breath.

'No!' he said emphatically.

After a further fifteen minutes the interview came to an inconclusive conclusion. Maxim was returned to his cell where his sister tore him off a strip about the rifle. Then she said pointedly.

'You knew the name, didn't you Jonny?'

'No, I didn't Sal. Honest.'

Back in his office, after being briefed on the interview, Blair asked for Tate and Trueman's views on how they should proceed.

'Well, sir, we could probably arrest Maxim for stealing a gun, or being in possession of an unlicensed firearm but that would be pointless, and, as Mrs Henshaw inferred, we have no forensic link to the murder. The problem for me is the person in the other car. Was he or she Donnelly's accomplice or Donnelly's murderer?'

'If an accomplice, why use two cars?' asked DS Trueman.

'Good point, Sergeant,' said Blair encouragingly.

'Do you think Maxim recognised the victim's name, sir?' continued Trueman, turning to Tate.

'Yes,' came the immediate response.

'Me too, sir,' agreed the DS.

'Very interesting,' said Blair. 'So, we need to know more about the dead man. A tricky one. My view is that we return Maxim to his status quo in Scargill Cottage, but that we put a shiny police car up there 24/7 with two armed officers as a deterrent, and we tell Tanner to find out everything he can about John Donnelly and any connection to Jonathan Maxim. Maxim goes nowhere from now on and only the Henshaws get access. Do we agree?'

Tate and Trueman both nodded.

Half an hour later a joyous, but handcuffed, Jonathan Maxim was sat next to his sister in the back of a police car travelling at speed back up the dale. Sally had rung ahead. As they moved slowly down the Scargill Cottage driveway, Tom Henshaw got out of his SUV ready to hug his wife in welcome and relief. DS Trueman removed the handcuffs and motioned all three into the cottage, with a final 'behave yourself' comment to Maxim. As the police car, driven by PC Craven, left and approached the screen of conifers, Trueman nodded across to two armed officers wearing full black assault kit and armed with semi-automatic carbines. They were there to be seen!

David Tanner had returned to Kettlewell with instruction from Blair. He didn't take instruction from the police well. He was MI5, after all. He was about to ring Dawson to bring him up to speed when he thought better of it. His day had not gone well. Maxim having a rifle had not been good! Not something to tell his boss, for sure. Tanner had his own contacts with the States and would find out about John Donnelly on his own.

CHAPTER 11

Although his three closest friends had been disposed of, Anton Davidov remained alive and well in Moscow looking after his sick mother in her small nondescript flat. He still had his own room, no longer filled with childhood toys and memories, but now kitted out with the hardware and software necessary for his job of work as Yevgeni Galerkin's chief hacker. His master had told him to stay there for his own safety but to find the man who had dared to steal so much money from the oligarch. Davidov reasoned that the thief may have got to Galerkin's account through his bank directly, but that this was not likely. The deaths of his friends could not be coincidental. He spent day after day trying to replicate what had been achieved, but in reverse. With access to Chamberland Asset Bank and Galerkin's account, and to his own and his dead friends' Swiss bank accounts and websites, he attempted to track backwards across the web from the likely hacked sites to the man he sought, or at least gain clues as to his identity and location. All this ended in failure.

The very fact that Davidov had got nowhere, with impenetrable firewalls and encryption, or sheer invisibility and security expertise, blocking his way, confirmed to Galerkin the involvement of the American or British intelligence services and, probably, GCHQ. It tied in with three out of the four of his most valuable assets being terminated on the same day. But the theft puzzled him. Why would the CIA or MI6 do such a trivial thing as to steal millions from a man who had billions? Also, if they knew about his team, and three were dead, then they knew about him. Yet he was still alive. It did not add up. Common sense demanded that he himself flee to Mother Russia, but he loved his London lifestyle and was a renowned and respected business man, a billionaire with his fingers in many pies, someone who was often seen on the back pages of national newspapers cheering from the stands. He decided that he would brazen it out, but from now on the security around him must be total. After all, would he really be any safer back in Moscow?

On the day after he had given up his search for a hacker who he now believed to be superior to himself, Davidov had a what if moment. He did not believe in coincidence. The deaths of his colleagues and the theft must be connected, but what if the man he sought had discovered the team of hackers and had then stumbled upon his master? Perhaps he was an opportunist, a common thief and had decided to steal from him? Davidov began to play once more. He concentrated on the month before the theft and hacked into the most popular search engines. He asked himself this question.

'Who had been finding out as much as they could about Yevgeni Galerkin?'

The answer was several thousand individuals, but he reasoned that most of them would be ordinary people or journalists or politicians. He was looking for someone who did not want to be found, someone who would try to block his way, someone not ordinary.

His search took him almost a week, but in the end, he found his way through a simple phone provider back to a single individual with unusually strong self-made security, not the sort you buy off the shelf from a high street store. No, he could not yet identify the person, or locate them, that would take more time, but he did discover something very interesting. That person played chess!

CHAPTER 12

It was a bright Sunday morning. David Tanner was aboard a high-speed train, travelling First Class to London from Leeds, sat well away from any prying eyes, studying his laptop screen. He was going through files on Michael Maxim that went back twenty years almost, searching for the name Donnelly. He had no luck. The single file on Jonathan Maxim was limited to the last five years or so, since the day that two British Secret Service officers had met their deaths at a safe house in London. Prior to that he had been regarded as a mere addendum to his father, not warranting his own paperwork. After an hour or so, annoyed by his lack of success, Tanner switched off the laptop and let thoughts play through his mind as he admired the countryside flashing by. One day he would buy himself a country retreat, in thirty years maybe!

He got into King's Cross just after one and went through the exit barriers. As rail passengers barged past him, he stood still, looking up at café tables that overlooked the concourse. He saw a single raised arm and recognised a man's face. He walked to the nearby escalator and was met at the top in silence by a firm friendly handshake. Tanner bought two espressos and joined the man at a small table in the noisy seating area.

'Good to see you, David, it's been a long time,' said the man in a matter-of-fact way.

'Yes, Tony. We only seem to see each other when one of us needs a favour, and this time it's me.'

The two men made small talk, but only for a minute or two, every few seconds checking around them to see whether they were being watched.

Then the man, an overly handsome American named Tony Masters, said:

'Well, David, on the basis that I owe you one, I've found out one or two things about the man in question. He used to work for the Agency. He retired two years ago after the death of his wife. She committed suicide. I take it he's dead.'

'Yes, we're trying to keep it under wraps. There is police involvement, but we should be able to shut it down.'

'Who killed him? I assume he didn't die of old age.'

'We don't know for sure yet,' replied Tanner. 'Do you know if he had any connections this side of the pond?'

'Workwise, he was mainly confined to the States. No contact with you Brits as far as I know. His wife was Irish though, so he might have been over here visiting maybe.'

'What was her maiden name?' asked Tanner.

The man hesitated.

'I don't know, David. Her first name was Maureen, if that's any help. I can find out if you think it's relevant.'

'Thanks, Tony. It could be. Another thing. What sort of work did he do for the Agency? Any elimination?'

'I can't tell you that, David, but let me put it this way, you wouldn't want to get in his way.'

'And he was fully retired? The last two years. No work from the side lines?'

'He was retired. Period. If he was doing something over here, it had nothing to do with us. No Agency work, guaranteed.'

'Thanks Tony. Fancy another espresso?' asked Tanner.

'Sure, but next time, David. Your turn to owe me one.'

The man stood and walked casually to the escalator and was gone. Tanner got himself another espresso and sat a while, mulling over what he had found out, or not. John Donnelly was ex-CIA but his presence in Wharfedale had nothing to do with the Agency. Tanner reasoned that he had probably been there to kill Jonathan Maxim. If so, either someone had paid him privately to do it or maybe he had a personal grudge. Tanner had no idea which and Superintendent Blair wasn't going to be too impressed with his progress.

An hour later David Tanner was back in First Class, hurtling north through the English countryside, daydreaming about his country retreat.

CHAPTER 13

Jonathan had got up early to make breakfast for everyone. It was only tea, toast, eggs and bacon, but he had made the effort. He was feeling a bit down now. Sally and Tom had been there for three days, and he'd enjoyed the time with his sister, chatting about mother and when they were young, the days at primary school together and the tricks they'd played on teachers. Mind you, Tom was starting to get on his nerves so maybe it was just as well that they were leaving today.

He knocked on mother's bedroom door.

'Breakfast, ready and on the table,' he shouted.

Sally emerged, glowing, followed by her yawning husband carrying two suitcases which he deposited on the floor near the front door.

They sat at the breakfast table in the kitchen.

'So, dear, you're going to behave. You have your medication and supplies for the week, and you are going to do exactly as Mister Tanner says. Hopefully, you'll have no visits from the police. I wouldn't chat to those two at the end of the drive if I were you. Just do your work.'

Jonathan frowned.

'Yes, yes, Sal,' he replied in irritation.

'It's for the best,' said Tom.

Jonathan glared.

'It's going to be fine, Jonny,' Sally continued. 'Tanner doesn't believe you killed Donnelly, and the police have no evidence. The armed policemen out there are here to protect you. When all this is cleared up, and your six months is over, you'll be free of them all. You really have no idea about this man Donnelly?'

'No, no, no,' came the petulant reply. 'But those armed guards aren't just for protection, Sal. What do you think they'd do if I ran down the drive towards them?'

He smiled. It was his sister's turn to glare.

Shortly after, Maxim watched from the kitchen window as the Henshaw's SUV was waved on through by the armed officers. The Inn at Buckden would be open today.

For the next two hours he worked at his workstation on queries from GCHQ, providing more details about Galerkin's hackers and their strategies and software for infiltrating defence facilities. He was ready for the final question that morning.

'Do you know yet who has been running them?'

'Yes,' was his reply.

Maxim had thought long and hard about this.

'I shall tell David Tanner.'

GCHQ's response was one of extreme annoyance but was countered by Maxim's final communication.

'This information is too sensitive!'

He turned off his workstation. He had decided to pass the buck, to make Tanner responsible for this knowledge. It would be up to him what he did with it.

After a snack of more toast and orange juice, Jonathan retrieved the laptop and phone hidden in his mother's bedroom. He was about to have an afternoon of music, Stravinsky perhaps, The Rite Of Spring being his favourite piece, when he received a request via his chess club app to play a game against Nightjar, a player who had challenged him several times before, and who was ranked twenty-third on the chess ladder.

'Challenge accepted. Spectrum available,' was Maxim's keyboard reply, using his own identifier.

The game started with standard openings, each sounding the other out with mock attack strategies. Jonathan had seen this all before. He was now ranked fifth and Nightjar's pattern of play was well known to him. However, after eleven moves he was one pawn down and was having to concentrate more than usual. Previous wins had taken less than twenty moves, but it was only after twenty-three moves today that Spectrum's win became inevitable to Maxim. He requested a five-minute time-out for a comfort break, not unusual in a long match. Jonathan was puzzled about his adversary's abilities today. Maybe he was being lucky, or maybe he was being helped by a chess machine, banned and frowned upon in the club, or maybe there was something else going on. Maxim made a dozen keystrokes and initiated his personal search software.

'Who are you, Nightjar?' he said to himself.

The game of chess continued for no more than five moves. Nightjar resigned and thanked Spectrum for the match.

Maxim stared at the pop-up box that appeared on his screen, courtesy of his software, as his adversary finished his message.

'Have a good day, Spectrum. I hope we can play again. Nightjar.'

'My pleasure, Anton Davidov, my pleasure,' said Maxim to himself, switching off the laptop.

He reached for his smartphone and keyed in Sally's number.

'I need to see Tanner, now Sally, it's urgent. Get him up here. We need to talk.'

She recognised the way her brother was speaking. There was no fear in his voice, and no anger. It was that steely professionalism that she had heard since childhood. It was the voice of her father, a man who loved a daughter, but a man who killed when necessary.

That same afternoon David Tanner received a two-word email from Tony Masters. 'Maureen Reagan,' was all it said. He then spent an hour or so going through back files on Michael and Jonathan Maxim, yet again, failing to find any mention of a Donnelly or a Reagan. His phone rang. Sally's voice was anxious, and she insisted that she go with him to Scargill Cottage.

As they drove down the driveway past the armed policemen, Jonathan emerged and held up his right hand. In the cottage, Maxim started to explain to Tanner the ins and outs of the work that he had been doing for GCHQ.

'Do you think that GCHQ keep me out of the loop!' said Tanner angrily. 'You identified four hackers situated in eastern Europe. Three are dead, courtesy of MI6. The fourth, called Davidov, is alive and now in Moscow. Tell me something I don't know.'

'Anton Davidov has found me through my provider, digitally if you like. He contacted me today but that does not mean that he knows my true identity or where I am located.'

Tanner was even angrier now.

'What do you mean, provider? Everything you do is through GCHQ!'

'Oh, Jonny!' said Sally. 'My brother has a mobile phone and laptop courtesy of Fred Denby, Mister Tanner.'

'Virgin bloody Mobile no doubt!' shouted Tanner. 'You'll be back in the clinic sooner than expected, Maxim.'

'No need for threats,' retorted Jonathan. 'I've merely been playing chess, online, that's all, no need to over-react. All the secret stuff has been on the workstation through GCHQ. I assure you, Davidov's knowledge is limited.'

'That's what you say. What if he is as good as you, or better?'

'Unlikely,' replied Maxim, 'but probably best to keep those handsome young officers out there though, just in case. There is something else that I need to tell you, more important, but I do not wish to tell GCHQ or the whole of MI5. I am going to trust you, Mister Tanner. I now know who has been running this team that has hacked into American, as well as British, defence. For your ears only, you might say. I leave it for you to decide who to tell. The man running this operation is very well-known, powerful and influential, even in this UK of ours. Yevgeni Galerkin, Mister Tanner, do you know of him?'

Tanner looked visibly shaken.

'Yes, I know of him. We investigated him when he bought properties in London and moved here. We gave him a clean bill of health, just a rich Russian enjoying the West.'

'Well, let me put it this way, Mister Tanner. Not MI5's finest hour. I am not wrong. That is why Davidov has been looking for me.'

Tanner was unconvinced by this last assertion but let it pass.

'OK,' he said, 'I need to think about what to do with this. Say nothing to anyone. Do not tell GCHQ. And another thing. You said that you didn't know of the American John Donnelly, although nobody believed you. What about Maureen Reagan, or any Reagan for that matter? She was Irish, his wife.'

Maxim smiled and then shook his head.

'You're right. Sis didn't believe me either. John Donnelly, no, Maureen Reagan, no. They mean nothing to me.'

Tanner and Sally looked into Jonathan's eyes as he spoke. This time they believed him.

CHAPTER 14

David Tanner's brain was beginning to spin. He had been encamped in the Fox and Hounds for three hours so far, sat not far from the comforting open fire provided by the sympathetic barman. He had gone through his notes and laptop files for the umpteenth time. He knew that he was getting nowhere and would have to run with an assumption or two. On the basis that an ex-CIA man would not choose to spend his retirement supplementing his pension by becoming a paid killer, he started to write.

One: John Donnelly was there to kill Jonathan Maxim and was killed by an accomplice who wanted to frame Maxim.

Two: He wanted to kill Maxim for personal reasons, linked to his or his father's activities or both.

MUST FIND CONNECTION BETWEEN DONNELLY AND MAXIM

He was unhappy with what he had written. This scenario was unconvincing, one of many he could have plucked out of the air. Donnelly certainly could have been a hired killer, or he could have been there only to observe, or he could have been duped into being there. But he was dead! Tanner had found no connection between the Maxims and this ex-CIA agent, and believed what Jonathan had told him, that the names Donnelly and Reagan meant nothing to him.

Nevertheless, he would run with it. If Donnelly had been there to kill, and had a personal grudge, then it had to be a big one. Who had been killed by the Maxims? Who had got in their way? Michael Maxim had headed up an SAS team working for MI6 in Iraq, and then a more ad hoc version in the UK, overseen by Tanner and MI5, although that now seemed like a bad joke gone wrong. Anybody who had been eliminated by Michael Maxim wasn't exactly an innocent. They were legitimate targets, terrorists or criminals, apart from the two MI5 officers at the safe house, and, and, the Garda officer!

What was the name of the Garda officer?

Tanner underlined the question twice.

One obvious thing that puzzled him was, why didn't he already know the answer?

Back in his Kettlewell cottage, Tanner read Michael Maxim's debrief to Dawson on his return from the debacle in Northern Ireland. He had read it several times before. He knew it backwards. He ought to! He himself had been the MI5 officer who had set up the covert operation, almost six years ago now, delegating full operational control to Michael Maxim, and it had gone pear-shaped. It was one of the main reasons why Tanner had ended up in Catterick, demoted to Army liaison. Maxim's brief had been to find and terminate James Cullen, the Irishman known by MI5 to have been responsible for the hit and run death of a Westminster MP. Cullen hadn't accepted the Good Friday agreement and never would. He was shunned by the very men that he'd fought alongside during the troubles and had gone rogue. MI5's view was that he must be eliminated, that he had few allies and that he wouldn't be missed. He was pinpointed as hiding alone in a small insignificant village. On the night when four men burst into a terraced house just half a mile north of the border, shots were fired and Cullen escaped out of the back door and over a wall, pursued by Michael Maxim and three others. A pursuit across open country in moonlight ended only minutes later when Cullen was shot dead as he ran across a narrow lane. His pursuers were now in Ireland! As shots rang out, a car screamed to a halt behind them. An unlucky overly brave Garda officer got out of his car and, pistol in hand, challenged the four men before him, faces blackened, dressed in khaki, each carrying an automatic weapon. Two seconds later he lay dead on the tarmac, illuminated by his own headlights. According to Michael Maxim, he had not realised that they were south of the border. Yes, it had been a mistake, but the job was done. Maxim had refused to say who shot the Garda officer or who had accompanied him.

'It's my team,' he had stated, 'and it's my responsibility.'

From that day on, Michael Maxim's days working for MI5 were numbered but his own termination had been botched by Tanner at the London safe house and he had escaped to hide in Wharfedale with his wife, son and daughter.

Tanner searched for the name of the Garda officer, but it was missing from the files. Strange, had it been redacted? But if so, why? Or just a lapse in detail? He went online and found Irish newspaper websites. He went through countless back issues until he found a headline. It was about the right date.

The headline read: Garda man killed on the border.

He read the article which suggested that a policeman had been shot by known terrorists on the run, and that one of them, James Cullen, was also dead. The name of the Garda officer was Denis Reagan.

'Yes!' shouted Tanner to an empty room.

He continued his search, scanning local newspapers for the two weeks following, until he came across the funeral he was looking for. There was a photograph of two distraught mourners.

Underneath the photograph was written:

Denis Reagan's wife Jane and his sister Maureen

Tanner considered what to do next. Should he tell Dawson? The police? He decided to confront Maxim with what he'd found out. He rang Sally Henshaw.

They arrived at Scargill Cottage late-afternoon and entered unannounced, finding Jonathan lying on the front room sofa, wearing headphones and listening to some podcast of trivia.

'I'm bored, Sal,' he offered.

'You won't be in a minute,' said Tanner bitingly.

'Oh, really, what news MI5?'

'I know the connection between you and John Donnelly.'

Maxim sat up, eyes narrowing, looking in the mood for a fight. Sally raised two hands and motioned her brother to be calm.

'Did you go to Northern Ireland with your father, Jonathan,' continued Tanner, 'to kill a terrorist? Did you kill an Irish policeman by mistake? Because, if you did, that policeman was the brother-in-law of John Donnelly. And Donnelly's wife committed suicide. Join the dots!'

Maxim looked upset with himself. If Tanner could believe it, it was almost as if he was about to cry. Jonathan glanced pleadingly at his sister.

'Yes, I was there. It just went all wrong. We got to Cullen, but it was the wrong side of the border. A mistake, that's all. The policeman, I never knew his name, but I didn't kill him. It was just a mistake. No-one to blame.'

'Did your father kill him?'

'Yes, father shot him with Cullen's own pistol. He'd just picked it up off the ground.'

'Clever,' said Tanner.

'No, it wasn't. Father just reacted instinctively, that's all. A mistake.'

'Don't be stupid! Your father was too good at his job to make a mistake. He got rid of the problem policeman and left a dead terrorist to take the blame.'

Jonathan stared at Sally. He shook his head. Tanner looked into the eyes of the brother, and then into the eyes of his twin sister.

Sally's expression never changed. Her eyes remained fixed on her brother's.

'It wasn't your fault, Jonny, and you were so young, my boy.'

'Don't make excuses for him,' said Tanner.

'What do you know, Tanner!' she shouted. 'Jonny was used by my father. He took him out of the London clinic even though he knew that he still wasn't well. He taught him to kill. He forced Jonny to work for him. It was abuse!'

'Abuse?' shouted Tanner.

'Yes, abuse,' Sally shouted back at him. 'In the end he tangled me in his web too and we had to escape to this God forsaken hole. Father attacked me when he was drunk one night, and died for it, but Jonny was only protecting me. And then I fell in love with a good man, an ordinary man. We deserve to be left alone, Mister Tanner, to have a life! What are you going to do now? You know why Donnelly came here. He's dead, and we didn't kill him. Find his killer. Then, leave us alone!'

'Yes, leave us alone!' shouted Jonathan. 'Sal is happy with Tom, living a good life, and I'm alright if she looks after me. I've done all that MI5 and GCHQ wanted. Go away, Mister Tanner!'

'Not until I've sorted this mess out,' said Tanner.

'Look after this boy of yours,' he mouthed at Sally before closing the front door as he left the cottage.

She sat down next to her brother and hugged him as he cried. After five minutes he suddenly stopped. He dried his eyes and said:

'I'm feeling upset, Sis, and angry, and I don't want to feel like this.'

CHAPTER 15

DCI Tate, arms folded, sat opposite his boss, next to David Tanner. Blair's secretary brought in three coffees and put one down in front of each man in silence. She left and Blair set the ball rolling.

'Your turn first, Alan. Any updates?'

'Not much, sir. Residue tests indicate that Donnelly did fire a handgun before meeting his demise. No more news from Doctor Jones or on the car that sped off towards Cray. No locals heard or saw anything of it apart from Mister Merriweather. Odd that. No cameras picked anything up around Skipton that night, but the driver could have headed north out of the dale.'

'David?' It was unusual, almost conciliatory, for Blair to use Tanner's first name. 'Any details on John Donnelly? Connections with Maxim?'

Tanner had thought a lot about what and what not to say.

'I contacted an American friend of mine. John Donnelly did work for the CIA, but he retired two years ago after the suicide of his wife. That suicide may be linked to the untimely death of her brother in Ireland a few years before. His death may be linked to the Maxims. So, John Donnelly might have had a motive to kill Jonathan Maxim, but there are still a lot of questions to answer.'

'Carry on, Mister Tanner. Fewer mays might help though,' said the unsmiling Superintendent.

'Well,' continued Tanner, 'I have no idea how Donnelly could have ever come across Jonathan Maxim, but Michael Maxim could have been known to him, either through activities in Iraq, or through connections with British intelligence. I have been told that Donnelly was solely US-based but I could have been spun a line. An interesting question is how well known is it that Michael Maxim is dead, and that he died here in Wharfedale? It never came out in the press, we saw to that, but reporters do have good connections with the police. To me, it is more likely that Donnelly was here to kill an already dead Michael Maxim, rather than his son, but I can't figure out how he could have connected Maxim to his brother-in-law's death. That was only known deep within MI5.'

'Only MI5 knew everything,' interrupted Tate. 'Any leak to the Americans must be your leak. What was it they used to say, careless talk costs lives?'

'I agree,' continued Tanner. 'If someone had leaked to the Americans or Donnelly about Michael Maxim and the death of the Garda officer in the last six months or so, then Donnelly might have known that Maxim was dead. Before that, no.'

Blair nodded, noting Tanner's own slip in mentioning a Garda officer.

'Yes, I see. So, either Donnelly thought Michael Maxim was alive or he knew that Jonathan Maxim was connected to his brother-in-law's death. Is that what you're saying?'

'Yes,' said Tanner, 'or I've been told lies for some reason or other. Maybe it's simpler than that. Maybe someone hired Donnelly to kill Jonathan Maxim, for their own reasons.'

'Hell,' said Tate, 'I'm glad I don't work in your world. Give me honest crooks and robbers any day!'

'I'm not sure that we can be much help to you, David,' said Blair. 'Are you certain in your own mind that Jonathan Maxim is innocent regarding the killing of John Donnelly?'

'Yes, sir, as certain as I can be, today,' replied Tanner.

'Then what do Skipton police do about Donnelly? Do we investigate? Do we go public?'

'I would advise against it, sir. I do not believe that you will find the person who did this. I think that he is a professional killer of some sort and is long gone. I would prefer it if you let us tackle this one on our own. We will tidy up for you and settle it with the Americans. I think we can do that.'

Tate was about to object but was silenced by his superior.

'I was hoping you might say that. Discussions I've had with the Chief Constable have suggested that that would be best for all of us. Scargill Cottage has had enough publicity in the last six months. I'd also suggest that Jonathan Maxim's time up there should come to an immediate end.'

'I'd rather it didn't, sir. There is another problem that has come to light, I cannot say what, but I'd be happy for your armed officers to leave the scene now. Maxim remains GPS-ed. He'll go nowhere.'

Blair and Tate exchanged glances, suspicious of Tanner's intentions.

'Do you believe that there will be another attempt on Jonathan Maxim's life, if that's what it was?'

'Perhaps, Superintendent.'

'It sounds to me that Maxim is the bait on the end of your hook,' said Tate starkly. 'You must be after a very big fish!'

Tanner denied himself a wry smile.

'What is Mister Dawson's view on all this?' asked Blair.

'He doesn't even know who's lying dead in your morgue, sir.'

'I'll expect your clean-up squad to arrive within twenty-four hours to remove the body. We shall close our file on this matter, for the time being. I wish you luck, David. You may need it.'

The two men shook hands, as did Tate, much to Tanner's surprise. David Tanner left Skipton police station and wondered if it was for the last time. He somehow doubted that. He drove his BMW the ten miles or so back to Kettlewell and parked in the Fox and Hounds car park. It was mid-afternoon on a cold March day. The pub was virtually empty. He sat with a double whisky in front of a roaring fire and thought. How the hell had Donnelly found his way to Wharfedale and Scargill Cottage? Was he his wife's avenging angel or just a hired killer? Or neither? After all, he was the one lying dead in the morgue. He thought about what to say to Dawson. He was the one man who had known everything about Michael Maxim. Wasn't he? And now there was another problem, Yevgeni Galerkin. Tanner finished his drink and ordered a pub meal. After a simple steak pie and chips, washed down with sparkling water, he went back to his cottage. So as not to overstep the mark he noted down what he was going to tell Dawson. He rang his boss's number.

Dawson seemed eager to hear what Tanner had to say but the conversation was surprisingly short. Tanner told him that the murdered man was John Donnelly, an ex-CIA agent, the brother-in-law of the Garda officer killed over six years before in Ireland by Michael Maxim's team, that he believed that Donnelly had mistakenly been there to kill an already dead man, and had been killed by someone, possibly an accomplice, who was far away by now. Dawson agreed to the clean-up squad and to putting a lid on the case with Skipton police. He would square it with the Americans somehow. Tanner was surprised at the lack of questioning from his boss. He also told Dawson about Davidov's chess match with Jonathan Maxim but made no mention of Yevgeni Galerkin.

'According to GCHQ, Jonathan Maxim now knows who has been running the team of hackers and has told you. Who is it, David?'

Tanner had been waiting for this question.

'The Russians, sir,' he replied.

'The Russians?' queried Dawson. 'You mean Moscow?'

'Yes, sir,' said Tanner, 'Maxim says that the four hackers were run from Moscow directly, to interfere with US-UK defence and test out our cyber security systems. He is going to continue with his work. He said that he can find out more. No point in eliminating the last hacker though, sir. Moscow will no doubt replace the team. Nevertheless, I do think that Maxim is being most useful to us and GCHQ.'

'Yes, very,' came the reply. 'He may get his freedom yet.'

The call ended between the two men. Tanner spent the next hour analysing every word.

CHAPTER 16

David Tanner rose early in his Kettlewell retreat so as to be ready for his expected delivery. The mirror told him, as ever, that he looked like a reasonably young executive-type, although the slight bulge under his jacket told a different story. As he tapped the holster with his right hand, a habit of his OCD nature since the safe house, there was a knock on the front door. He opened it to see a familiar face.

'Good morning, sir, will you sign for this?'

'Thanks, Graham, I see we haven't progressed to a tablet yet.'

'No, sir, still pen and paper. Nothing gets lost that way.'

Tanner duly signed the chit. The man gave a mock salute, smiled and went on his way, a fast car ride back to London.

Tanner carried the long black bag into the tiny front room and unzipped it to reveal the contents.

'Yep, that should do,' he said to himself.

He zipped the bag back up and carried it outside, placing it in the boot of the BMW. Fifteen minutes later he was climbing out of Cray. A police car travelling downhill and carrying two armed officers flashed its lights as it squeezed past him on the narrow winding road. Their vigil at Scargill Cottage had come to an end. As Tanner turned right onto the driveway between the conifer screen, he saw a quadbike tearing towards him. Jonathan Maxim hit his brakes and came to an immediate halt in front of the BMW. He jumped off the quadbike and raised his right fist into the air.

'They've gone MI5!' he shouted. 'Victory!'

He burst out laughing, got back on the quadbike and hurtled it at his garden wall before braking heavily once more. He got off and stood with arms folded, waiting.

To emphasise the contrast, Tanner drove sedately down the drive and parked next to the quadbike.

'There's a present for you in the boot,' he said calmly as he emerged from the car. 'Bring it in.'

Jonathan's boyish curiosity took over. He strode across to the car, retrieved the black bag and carried it into the cottage, followed by Tanner.

Jonathan unzipped the bag. Inside was a pair of binoculars, a stiletto throwing knife, an automatic pistol, a high-powered rifle with telescopic sights, and a supply of ammunition. He stared at Tanner in astonishment.

'I don't get it, MI5. What's going on? You dislike me, you don't trust me, you think I'm a cold-blooded killer, and now you give me this bag of goodies. Why?'

'Listen to me carefully, Jonathan. I do not believe that you had anything to do with Donnelly's death. He came here to kill you. Of that I am sure. His threat is over, but someone else may come. That someone else might be linked to Donnelly, or to Galerkin, or even to MI5, God forbid. We will wait this one out. If no-one comes, then good, but if they do, you need to be able to protect yourself. You understand?'

'Of course,' replied Maxim.

'Are you sure you're not underestimating Davidov, Jonathan? Could he have identified you and this location?'

'It is possible,' admitted Maxim.

Tanner nodded slowly.

'If he tries another game of chess, be careful, and try to assess how much he knows if you can. Maybe provoke him, but don't give him information.'

'Who knows about Galerkin?' asked Maxim.

'Just you and me and your sister. I told my boss that the hackers were run by the Russians, that's all, and that may be the truth of it. If so, MI6 killing a few hackers was pointless, but if Galerkin is working independently, for money or ideology, or for who knows what reason, then eliminating him might be necessary. He appears to be trying hard to find you, Jonathan, a mere hacker, to kill you maybe. Why is that do you think?'

'No idea, except that we kill his men, so he kills ours.'

'Maybe,' said Tanner, unconvinced. 'Anyway, about Donnelly, how could he have found you? And, by you, I mean you or your father. He could have been the target if Donnelly didn't know that he's dead.'

'Only through the police or MI5. No-one else found out where we were.'

'Think Jonathan. Is there anyone else who knew you were here? Remember, Donnelly's motive was probably the Garda officer.'

Jonathan began to fidget nervously, self-confidence draining.

'No, it couldn't be, but father and I did see the other two guys, once after we'd come here, at a sort of reunion, a few drinks in a pub near Catterick. Father got a bit drunk as usual and a bit talkative, but it was only Ken and Davy, the two with us when we got Cullen. They wouldn't talk. Ex-SAS look after each other.'

'Well, either there's a hell of a mole in all this, police or MI5, or Donnelly got it from someone else. Tell me about the other two. Where are they now?'

'No chance, Mister Tanner. Father's been dead over four years, and I've been holed up here. No contact with anybody.'

Maxim told Tanner all he knew about Ken and Davy, which was precious little, just their full names and rank in the SAS. It was enough.

Tanner left Jonathan to play with his new toys and drove down to Buckden. It was lunchtime in The Inn, and it was heaving. For once, the pub was open, and the locals and walkers were making the most of it. Tanner sat with a pint of John Smiths watching Tom Henshaw being his usual genial host at the bar while Sally, Katie and a new girl, Hazel, tore about, preparing and serving steak pies, curry and sandwiches to all and sundry. At around three o'clock, things became less hectic, and Sally took a seat opposite Tanner. He explained his visit to her brother.

'You've given him what!' she shouted.

The bar fell completely silent and all eyes fixed on the MI5 officer. Ten seconds of silence ended, and the hubbub restarted. Tanner managed to placate the landlady, for that was all she was to the locals, and kept going as best he could. When she realised that he was trying to protect her brother her mood softened.

'You see, Mrs Henshaw, if this all works out then Jonathan is home free, and you will get your life back.'

'But this is so dangerous, David,' she said. 'Maybe I should be up there with him. I can shoot a gun.'

'No, stay clear, except for the usual. I'll join him soon.'

He asked if she knew anything about two men who worked with her father, but she didn't. After taking three hours over his one pint, Tanner went back to Kettlewell where he searched files and databases for current information about Kenneth Mason and David Price. Photographs of the two ex-SAS men told Tanner that he himself had met them more than once in Iraq all those years ago when running covert ops for MI6. Both men were dead.

Kenneth Mason had died two years earlier of a major stroke at the age of forty-seven. As for Price, he had been found shot dead in his own flat in Nottingham, only one month ago. The flat had been ransacked. According to the file, police suspected that a robbery had gone wrong but had made little progress with the case and had no suspects. So, three out of the four men responsible for the death of the Garda officer, Denis Reagan, were themselves dead. Tanner surmised that John Donnelly had somehow found out, perhaps through a leak between MI5 and the CIA, that Michael Maxim's team had been assigned to kill Cullen and had ended up killing his brother-in-law. Maxim was dead, Mason was dead, and Donnelly killed Price, with only Jonathan to deal with. After all, revenge is a powerful motive. Tanner knew that he could never prove this supposition now and, it could be completely wrong!

100

CHAPTER 17

The following morning Tanner was again on a fast train to King's Cross. He had sent a short message to Tony Masters the night before. It read:

Tony. Need to discuss JD. Need more info. Have important trade.

This time Tanner arrived first. He knew that Masters had been purposefully helpful at their last meeting, providing him with just enough information to start piecing together Donnelly's backstory. Tony was nearly an hour late and Tanner was on his second espresso by then, bored at examining the faces around him.

'Hello David,' came a voice from behind, the CIA man with a coffee in hand. He sat down and the two exchanged their usual pleasantries before getting down to business. Both were more relaxed than at their previous meeting.

'I'm guessing you're late because you had to clear what you can tell me with your boss,' said Tanner. This was met with a smile by the American.

'Correct, David. It depends on your trade. Is it good?'

'Very,' replied Tanner.

There had always been trust between the two men. Over the years, each had done the other a favour, more than once.

'What do you want to know about Donnelly?'

'Did he ever work in Iraq? Did he ever come across Michael Maxim?'

There was no look of surprise on Tony's face.

'Yes,' came the rapid response.

'Donnelly worked in Baghdad, helping the Iraqis guard against the theft of museum treasures. You might say he was a security adviser. Michael Maxim came under suspicion, but David, you know that, you were there. We are aware that a priceless artefact was recently returned to the Iraqis by the British. You have something to do with that?'

Tanner nodded.

'Michael Maxim is dead, Tony,' he said. 'I think Donnelly turned up to kill a dead man, but someone got to him.'

The American's face looked shocked at this news.

'We never sanctioned the operation,' he said quickly, 'and what I told you last time was the truth. Donnelly retired. No contact with the Agency in two years.'

'Have you any idea how Donnelly could have got wind of any ops over here involving Maxim, five or six years ago?'

'That's not what you really want to know, David. This is all about Donnelly's brother-in-law, the Irish policeman.'

Tanner stared into the face of a man he thought he trusted and still wanted to.

'Level with me, Tony. You know a hell of a lot more about this than I do.'

'I don't know everything, David, but the Irish never believed that Denis Reagan was shot by Cullen because they knew that Cullen wasn't shot by Reagan. Someone else had to be there. The policeman's gun was never fired. Intelligence and common sense told them that it was the British. It got hushed up because of the politics, the peace process.'

'But that doesn't explain how Donnelly found out.'

'He knew it was the British because Irish Intelligence told the CIA.'

'How could he know that Maxim's men killed his brother-in-law?'

'That's easy, maybe. The op was shared information between you and us. The Agency was told that Cullen was to be eliminated by MI5, Dawson's department. After all, we were the ones who told MI5 that he was the lone wolf who killed the Member of Parliament. The thinking is that Donnelly was high enough up in the Agency to dig around and piece it all together. The big problem was that he went nuts after his wife killed herself. His retirement was necessary from the Agency's point of view.'

'What a tangled sodding web,' said Tanner. 'Thanks, Tony.'

'What's your trade, David? It had better be good.'

'It is!' said Tanner, smiling at last. 'You remember the cyber attacks last year on both sides of the pond, when NATO defence network software was shut down for three days and all hell broke loose? I know who did it, but it's got to be sealed, Tony, zero leaks, in-house only, not even back to us, until I give you the all clear. Deal?'

Tony stood up and walked away. Tanner watched as Masters took out his mobile phone and had a conversation that lasted no more than a minute. On his return, he sat back down and stated:

'Deal. Who?'

'It was a coordinated team of four hackers, as good as any we've got, almost. The man running them was Yevgeni Galerkin.'

'We were getting close,' said Tony, looking unsurprised, 'but my bosses had it down as just another annoyance from our friends in Moscow.'

'Maybe it was,' said Tanner, 'but the hackers were paid directly from Galerkin's funds.'

'What are you going to do about Galerkin?'

'That's another reason for our discussion, Tony. I'm telling you about Galerkin, but no-one else. He has influence over here and it worries me. Billionaires have what we call clout. Frankly, I don't trust anyone and Galerkin may well be beyond my reach. But not yours!'

'I understand,' said the CIA man with extreme seriousness. 'I will put what you say to my boss. It's been good seeing you again, David.'

He shook hands with Tanner, the usual courtesy between them, and hurried away.

As Tanner dozed on the train back north, Jonathan Maxim was signing off with GCHQ for the day, realising that he was being asked to do less now. They were catching up and he figured that their need for his expertise was diminishing. That worried him.

He switched from his workstation to his laptop and decided to stay in his own room for most of the day. It was safer. He could keep glancing at the security camera screen. He keyed in a request to play chess against anyone in the club and got an immediate response from Nightjar.

'Hiya, Spectrum. It would be a privilege to test myself against number five on the ladder again.'

Their game started in a standard fashion with Spectrum accepting Nightjar's opening gambit, but to Jonathan's surprise, white's pawn sacrifice was never retrieved, and Nightjar resigned after fourteen moves.

'Well played Nightjar. Unlucky. Good game. I work from home but will return to staring out of my window.'

The onscreen reply was swift.

'Ah, work, work, work! What do you see out of your window? I see a boring cityscape.'

'A sea view, but dull and cold today. And your cityscape?'

'Dull and cold too.'

'Not even a square of red in the sky?'

It seemed like an age before Nightjar responded.

'Ha ha. I see that we are playing games, my British enemy. I am safe here in my world but three of my friends are dead. My best friends! Are you safe I wonder? I shall leave you with my favourite quotation. We shall not play again.'

The game was over.

The quotation appeared on Jonathan's screen.

When work is a pleasure, life is a joy! When work is a duty, life is slavery.

Early that evening, Tanner arrived. He drove his BMW around the side of the cottage and parked next to the quad bike in front of the ramshackled outbuilding. He carried a large box into the cottage kitchen and shouted through to Jonathan.

'I've brought more supplies.'

Maxim was surprised by Tanner's seemingly relaxed behaviour. He hadn't phoned ahead. He hadn't driven cautiously up to the cottage or emerged armed and ready for anything. He'd just turned up with groceries like a kindly uncle!

'What news, MI5?' asked Jonathan rhetorically as he emerged from his den.

'Oh, nothing much,' said Tanner with a smile, 'except that Donnelly certainly knew, or knew of, your father in Iraq. It all fits, now, I think. He came to kill your father, the man you killed. Ironic, eh.'

'Really?' replied Jonathan. 'You are so good at irony.'

Tanner let the remark pass.

'I looked into your two colleagues, Ken and Davy. One died naturally and one was shot dead in his flat in Nottingham a month ago. My guess is that Donnelly killed him and then came to get you, or your father, or both of you.'

Jonathan seemed unfazed by the news.

'Still no clues to who killed Donnelly, though?'

'No,' said Tanner.

'I've been playing chess today, against Nightjar. It was our last game. I won the game and then teased him a little. He hates me, I think. He will know that I work for GCHQ or MI5 or MI6. That is obvious. He knows that I am British. But there is more that he knows.'

Tanner bit his bottom lip with apprehension.

'Follow me, MI5.'

Jonathan led him into his room, stood in front of his laptop screen and pointed at the quotation.

When work is a pleasure, life is a joy! When work is a duty, life is slavery.

Tanner was puzzled.

'Look at the screen, Mister Tanner. Davidov asked me how safe I felt and left me with this, his favourite quotation.

'So what?'

'You don't know much about Russian writers, Mister Tanner?'

'What do you think?' said Tanner. 'Whose quote is it?'

Jonathan grinned.

'The quotation is from Maxim Gorky, Mister Tanner, Maxim Gorky.'

CHAPTER 18

Tom Henshaw had just finished some hoovering and dusting and was tidying the bar at The Inn when he heard someone turn into the car park at the back of the pub. He walked out of the back door into Spring sunshine to be met by a small man with a dishevelled look about him. The man held out his right hand. For some reason, the offer of a handshake was ignored by the usually gregarious landlord.

'What can I do for you, sir?' said Tom. 'It's a bit early for a drink. Do you want to book a room?'

It was nine o'clock.

'No, Mister Henshaw, I was hoping to chat to your wife.'

'And why would that be, Mister?'

'Davies,' replied the man. 'I'm a reporter with The Post. I'd just like to hear her side of the story, what happened at Scargill Cottage.'

'What do you mean?' said Tom.

'Come off it, Mister Henshaw. Mrs Law's death, I'm sure you're aware of the rumours.'

Tom was wary of making a mistake with what he said. Better to get Sally. She was the bright one of the two. He turned on his heels and shouted up at Sally's open bedroom window.

'I'll be right down, Tom,' she shouted back. 'Get Mister Davies a coffee, if he'd like one.'

The reporter smiled at his success. Five minutes later Sally walked calmly into the bar. Davies gave a noticeable intake of breath. No-one ever expected the landlady to look like that. She sat down and glared at him while Tom retreated to the kitchen.

'Well, Mister Davies, what do you really want? As far as I am concerned, the tragic death of my mother at her cottage was an accident. I'm sure you know that.'

The reporter responded with an exaggerated look of surprise.

'Mrs Henshaw, when your mother met with her tragic accident, as you call it, the police instituted a nationwide search for yourself and a Mister Jonathan Maxim, someone we now believe to be your brother. That is hardly what Skipton police usually do when an accident occurs! After that, everything went quiet and, if I can put it this way, all newspapers were warned off. National security, we were told. From my paper's point of view, that won't do, especially when we've heard that your brother has returned to Scargill Cottage and you're back here running the pub as if nothing ever happened.'

'All I can say is that my mother's death was investigated by the police and found to be accidental. I have nothing else to add.'

'Very well, Mrs Henshaw. Then perhaps your brother would be able to tell me more. You don't mind if I go up there to interview him?'

Sally was becoming nervous.

'That is not possible,' was her response. 'My brother is a recluse. He wishes to be left alone. It would be extremely unwise of you to disturb him.'

'That sounds like a threat,' countered Davies.

'No threat,' said Sally forcing a smile.

'You see, Mrs Henshaw, now that you've confirmed that Jonathan Maxim is indeed your brother, and we know that your mother was Mrs Law, can you tell me how it is that Sally Law's brother is Jonathan Maxim. An odd family, eh?'

'Half-brother, Mister Davies.'

'Nicely done, Mrs Henshaw.' The reporter grinned triumphantly. 'Well, I'd be grateful if you would have a word with your brother. I would really like to talk to him. There's big money available for a good story. You see, we don't like cover ups, especially government cover ups.

Think about it. We could meet on neutral ground if you'd rather. I'll get back to you in a couple of days.'

Davies looked down at his cold coffee and downed it in one.

'Think about it,' he said again, and left the pub.

Sally did not move from her chair. She heard a car pull away from the car park and turn left back down the dale. Tom came through to her.

'What are you going to do, Sal?' he asked.

'I don't know, Tom,' she said. 'It's too dangerous to tell Jonny. Another problem for Tanner I think.'

Jonathan was in his room, doing GCHQ work, when Sally phoned Tanner on his mobile and told him about Davies. Tanner was immediately suspicious. Yes, MI5 had put a lid on the Peter Wilson case, and on the shooting of Mrs Law, but both deaths occurred over six months ago. It seemed too coincidental that a meddling reporter should turn up now.

'So, he works for the Post, Davies you say?'

'Yes, Davies.'

'Describe him, age etcetera,' said Tanner.

'He is in his early fifties, I'd say, thinning on top, a small man, inconsequential looking, Yorkshire accent. I didn't like him.'

'Obviously not!' said Tanner. 'I'll check him out and get back to you. I won't tell your brother, not yet at least.'

'Thanks David,' Sally said, much to David Tanner's surprise.

Tanner went into the kitchen and shouted through to Jonathan.

'Do you want a coffee!'

'Yes, MI5,' came the reply.

Tanner carried two mugs of instant into Jonathan, pushing the door open with his right foot. It had been left ajar.

'Did you get any of that?' he asked.

The two of them, each regarding the other as a sworn enemy, were having to get on with each other and it was starting to happen.

'Yes, MI5. Some annoying reporter is nosing about. He's seen Sis and wants to see me.'

'Correct, Jonathan, but we need to check him out. Use those skills of yours. Ignore GCHQ for an hour. Verify Davies, reporter for the Post. I need to see a photograph. Try staff lists.'

'Yeh, yeh, yeh,' said Jonathan in a bored fashion. 'If I can hack into GCHQ, I think I can manage this little task of yours.'

Tanner retreated to the kitchen, closing the door behind him. He went into the front room and watched daytime television with the sound down, mulling over his views on his boss, Dawson, and his boss's views on him, still not knowing how much he was going to tell him when next they talked. Less than forty minutes later, Jonathan bounced into the room.

'Edward Davies, aged fifty-two, born in Huddersfield, degree in journalism at York, unmarried, joined The Post in 2008, height five foot five, job title Investigative Reporter, do you want to see his passport photo?'

Before Tanner could answer, Maxim held up an A4 sized photograph of Davies and said:

'He's genuine, I think. Agreed?'

'Agreed,' said Tanner as Maxim returned to GCHQ work in his room.

After fifteen minutes thinking time, Tanner rang Sally. He suggested that, whenever the reporter got back to her, she should agree to Jonathan meeting him, in the bar of the Lion at Cray, at midday on a day of the reporter's choosing.

'That's crazy!' shouted Sally.

'No, it isn't,' replied Tanner. 'There's no way that the guy knows what Jonathan looks like. I will be Jonathan for the day. Don't worry. He won't bother us again. If it goes wrong, I'll put the frighteners on him.'

CHAPTER 19

Over the next few days Tanner was starting to tire of nursemaiding Jonathan Maxim in the confines of Scargill Cottage. He was extremely bored, waiting for something to happen. Sally turned up to check on her brother and to do household tasks for him, and to make sure he took his medication, but she hardly talked to Tanner. He felt as though he was still regarded as the enemy, despite all he'd done, or maybe because of all he'd done. He couldn't quite work that one out. So, when he received a phone call late one evening from his boss to meet him the next day in Leeds, he was initially pleased at the prospect of a change of scenery.

'Do you know the Adelphi, just over the bridge, near the Tetley Gallery? We'll have a pub lunch and a drink and a quiet chat.'

It was the quiet chat that bothered him. Dawson rarely strayed from his office in Whitehall. Tanner thought carefully about what his boss knew or didn't know. He hadn't exactly kept him up to speed with what was going on.

The following morning Tanner drove into Skipton and got the train to Leeds. The Adelphi was only a five-minute walk from the station. As he walked through the narrow entrance door towards the bar, a voice shouted from a small room to his right. Dawson was sat alone.

'Close the door behind you, David. I've had a word with the landlord. We've got the room to ourselves for an hour.'

'That's good, sir,' said Tanner with a degree of sarcasm. 'Nice pub, very traditional, 1930s décor, I'd say, by the look of the wall tiles and paintings and the greens and browns.'

'I've ordered steak pie and chips and a bottle of red,' said his boss. 'Satisfactory?'

'Yes, sir, you know me rather too well.'

'Perhaps not as well as I might,' came the rapid reply, as two girls brought in their meals and left hurriedly.

David Tanner prepared himself for the hit that he knew must be coming and did not bother to reply.

'So, David,' began Dawson, 'the idea was that Jonathan Maxim would spend an innocuous six months in Wharfedale teaching GCHQ all his trickery and solving problems for them. And then we would decide what to do with him. You were there to make sure that nothing went wrong. But John Donnelly, and yes, before you ask, I met him several times on visits across the pond, he turns up here and ends up dead, but you insist that Maxim, rather good at making people dead, is not the man responsible. I have been speaking to Superintendent Blair who tells me that all is well, everything has been cleaned up, and that we will never know who killed the CIA man. Correct?'

'Probably, sir.'

'Probably!' exclaimed Dawson. 'What's even more startling is that the Agency has been in touch with me. You are not the only one with friends in the CIA. Apparently, you indicated to them that it might be a good idea to terminate a very influential Russian living in London, a Russian who, I am informed, has been asking some very important people about the possibility of dual citizenship, now that he's invested several billion pounds in the City, supported endless charities and runs some football club or other.'

'But he's a traitor, sir.'

'He's a bloody Russian,' said Dawson, 'of course he's a traitor.'

'You recall the four gold-star hackers, sir, responsible for all those cyber attacks on defence sites last year?'

'Yes,' said his boss, 'senility hasn't quite set in yet. They were run by our friends in Moscow.'

'Not exactly, sir. It was Yevgeni Galerkin who was running them. Jonathan Maxim has traced their money directly back to him. Galerkin was paying them from his own funds.'

'We'd better eat our food,' said Dawson in a matter-of-fact way.

The two men were silent for the next ten minutes. Dawson placed his knife and fork side by side on his plate, drank his glass of wine and then refilled it from the bottle in front of him. Tanner had already finished his food.

'As you know, David, we had our suspicions of Galerkin some time ago, but we can't just have him eliminated on Maxim's say so, nor can the Americans, even if Maxim has irrefutable proof. I shall deal with this matter myself, with the Minister's approval. There is no need for you to be involved. It is likely that pressure can be put on Galerkin to behave. If he chooses not to, he will be sent back to Moscow and I do not think he likes the lifestyle over there.'

'I believe that he's trying to get to Maxim, sir, to kill him.'

'Why would Galerkin bother himself with an annoying geek?' queried Dawson.

'The annoying geek tracked down four hackers and three were eliminated. The fourth has found Maxim online but may not know his location.'

'Yes, for MI6 to get heavy was a mistake, but Galerkin could replace three hackers with less hazard to himself, surely? Maybe it's just the fourth hacker who's after Maxim.'

'I hope you're right, sir. I'm babysitting just in case.'

'Maxim's usefulness may be coming to an end. Perhaps we should let him take his chance.'

This last phrase angered Tanner but he didn't show it and merely nodded. Dawson returned to the subject of Donnelly's death.

'You believe Donnelly was in Yorkshire to kill Michael Maxim, not knowing of his demise, for personal reasons, is that right?'

'Yes, sir.'

'Run it by me again, David. What was his grudge against Maxim?'

'I believe that Donnelly found out that Michael Maxim was responsible for the death of his brother-in-law, the Garda officer in the operation to kill James Cullen that went wrong, sir.'

Dawson smiled and purposefully displayed an element of surprise at this assertion by raising his eyebrows.

'As I've said before, David, we could have all swung for that one. I told you what to do, you told Maxim what to do, and Maxim strayed across the border and shot somebody he shouldn't have shot. Tell me, this brother-in-law, I'm rather confused.'

Tanner was visibly irritated. He couldn't tell whether his boss knew everything already or knew precious little.

'Donnelly left the Agency two years ago after his wife committed suicide. I think that she'd got depressed about her brother's killing, the Garda officer, and when Donnelly got the chance, when he retired, he went after the man who caused it all, Michael Maxim.'

Dawson nodded but then smiled again.

'Two things,' he said. 'First, how did Donnelly find out who killed the Garda officer? It was assumed by the Irish police that Cullen shot him. The ballistics proved it.'

'No idea,' replied Tanner, lying. 'And second, sir?'

'Second, David. What wife?'

'What do you mean, what wife, sir?'

Dawson sat back in his chair, clasped his hands behind his head, and gave a wide grin, disturbing Tanner instantly.

'You see, David, as I mentioned earlier, I came across Donnelly, admittedly years ago, over in the States, and as far as I can recall, he batted for the other side, if you get my meaning! I suggest you need to do more homework.'

Just then, the landlord, a larger than life efficient mein host, entered the room.

'Finished in here yet, Mister Dawson? I've got a party booked for two o'clock.'

'Yes, definitely finished,' replied Dawson. 'Do I owe you any money?'

'No, sir, your payment was more than generous, thank you. If you need the Adelphi again, please get in touch.'

'Oh, I will,' said Dawson as he stood up. 'Well, David, I'm off to the Gallery for the afternoon. My train is at five. I suggest you continue to clear up the mess. Let me know whodunnit!'

He turned away and walked out.

Tanner stared at the landlord who looked confused.

'A double whisky and a pint of Speckled Hen, please,' he said calmly, handing the landlord a twenty-pound note. 'I'll come through to the bar.'

CHAPTER 20

Tanner got back to Scargill Cottage late in the afternoon after his Adelphi chat with Dawson. Jonathan watched his car approaching out of the kitchen window as he made himself a soup and sandwich snack. Boredom was starting to take its toll on him too. GCHQ demanded less and less from him and he feared being taken away, back to the Isle of Man clinic or some other institution. Confinement away from his sister was probably what he feared the most. He had always relied on his mother, or his father, or Sally, to look after him. He knew that he wasn't what people called normal, whatever that meant. His darkest days had been when he was a student at Cambridge, a place full of not normal people, but, despite his obvious brilliance to those around him, he was treated as a weird outsider. On one occasion an extremely unwise fellow computer science student teased Jonathan for his 'odd dress sense', a poor joke in less enlightened times. Jonathan hit him once and walked away. The result was two broken ribs. Soon after, he left Cambridge.

Tanner walked into the cottage and shouted.

'Got another job for you.'

Jonathan's spirits immediately picked up.

'Great, MI5,' he shouted back. 'Ethical hacking, I trust.'

He tucked into his sandwich as Tanner strode into the kitchen.

'I'm afraid it is, for once. Standard US databases, they should be publicly available. I need to know if John Donnelly was really married, his wife's maiden name, and whether she is dead, and, if she is, how she died. And, if you can, was Donnelly batting for the other side, as my boss called it? In short, find out everything you can about him.'

'I thought you knew all this,' said Maxim.

'Just do it, please.'

Jonathan beamed a smile. He couldn't recall a please before.

Tanner sat and ate the Chinese takeaway that he'd picked up in Skipton on his way back, before he'd called in at his own cottage in Kettlewell to collect a few things that Graham had left for him. He would sign for them another time. For the following hour he walked the perimeter of the Scargill Cottage smallholding, merely a paddock in front and a field behind, planting small cameras, each with its own transmitter and microphone, every fifty yards or so. Perhaps he was being too cautious, getting too nervous, feeling too vulnerable up there. He wanted more security, not just the cottage cameras focused down the drive. He then set up a receiver and monitor in the front room. A curious Maxim came through to see what he was up to.

'Oh, very nice, MI5, very high tech.' he said. 'You must be getting scared.'

'Just careful,' countered Tanner. 'Have you got the info on Donnelly?'

'Yes,' said Jonathan, glancing down at a sheet of paper. 'It looks as expected to me.'

'And you used publicly available databases?'

'Well, not exactly,' replied Maxim. 'That would have been too dull, so I thought I'd interrogate the CIA's own file on him. No worries. They'll never know.'

Tanner shook his head and swore.

'So?' he said.

'So,' said Jonathan, 'according to his file, he retired two years ago aged 55, wife Maureen, maiden name Reagan, hanged herself shortly before, after spending two years being treated for depression. The couple were childless. The file indicates an indiscretion early in Donnelly's career regarding a male colleague. His marriage had been welcomed by the Agency. So, I assume he batted for both sides, or wanted it to appear that way.'

'Excellent, Jonathan,' said Tanner. 'I'm guessing that there was a hell of a lot of guilt inside Donnelly when his wife killed herself. The thesis still stands. He came here to kill your father.'

'Perhaps,' said Jonathan with a grin, 'and, according to the file, he knew father in Iraq.'

'Yes, I know,' said Tanner, 'but they were on different sides sometimes. Remember the small golden carriage, the priceless Persian antiquity that your father stole from the Baghdad Museum? Donnelly was responsible for security there. The Americans were none too pleased.'

'But I did give the toy back to the Iraqi nation. Nice of me, I thought.'

'Yes, Jonathan, so good of you to return stolen goods. Anyway, none of this tells us anything about who killed Donnelly, but at least I'm satisfied why he was here.'

'Maybe,' replied Jonathan, 'maybe.'

CHAPTER 21

In his late forties, handsome, six-foot two, besuited in dark blue with white shirt and red tie, and brogues, John Dawson looked every inch the essence of a high ranking civil servant as he strode confidently through the revolving doors into the Mayfair six-storey block of flats, flats owned by none other than Yevgeni Galerkin. He was met by an attractive receptionist and observed carefully by two men, equally as imposing as himself, one situated to the right of the reception desk and the other standing outside lift doors well to the left. This lift was for the private use of Galerkin who occupied the top floor of the block. There was another lift for mere mortals in the corner to the right. Dawson smiled at the receptionist.

'My name's Anderson, from the Home Office. I have an appointment to see Mister Galerkin at two o'clock.'

'Have you proof of identity, sir?' came the obvious question.

Dawson produced a Home Office staff identification card and a letter on appropriately headed paper detailing his appointment.

'Thank you, sir,' said the efficient young woman, pointing Dawson towards the lift to his left.

As he approached it, the security man took a step towards him and asked politely to frisk him. 'Purely routine, sir,' he offered.

The man pressed a button and the lift doors opened. Thirty seconds later Dawson emerged on the top floor where another security man frisked him for a second time. The man spoke into a microphone on his lapel and a door opposite opened. As Dawson entered the room, he realised that he was walking into another world, a world of opulence, but a world that, from his point of view, lacked taste. Everywhere was bling. Galerkin got up from behind the biggest marble-topped desk that he had ever seen and held out his right-hand which Dawson duly grasped.

'Take a seat, Mister Anderson,' said Galerkin in an almost caricature Russian accent. 'I hope that the Home Office has good news.'

'Indeed, Mister Galerkin,' replied Dawson, glancing behind him to see two very fit looking men, hands clasped behind their backs, standing to attention either side of the doorway. Dawson sat down opposite the Russian and adopted a relaxed pose with a smile.

'First, I must point out that immigration policy and citizenship law is currently under review,' continued Dawson. This was met with somewhat of a glare from the Russian.

'However, we do now have all the paperwork in place and have established that your mother was, as you claimed, British by birth, born in Manchester in 1936, and the Home Office is minded to give positive support to your application for dual citizenship, with one or two provisos.'

Galerkin nodded approval.

'And what would these provisos entail? More billions on the London Stock Exchange, perhaps, or a Premier League title?'

He glanced at his security guards who laughed obediently.

'I would prefer complete privacy to discuss such matters, if that is possible.'

Galerkin nodded and the two guards left the room.

'Please continue, Mister Anderson.'

Dawson's voice did not alter, still affecting the manner of a civil servant, though his words told a different tale.

'It has come to the attention of Her Majesty's Government that you have been financing four very valuable assets working in the Defence sector, both here and in the United States, and it is felt that you should desist from such investments.'

Galerkin leaned forward and, in a voice that even Dawson found unnerving, said:

'Who are you really, Mister Anderson? Home Office? No!'

Dawson gazed theatrically around the room.

'What a marvellous office you have!' he stated. 'And a marvellous London lifestyle. And a marvellous reputation, well respected, adored by a certain section of the populace. So easily lost, all of it, but no doubt Mother Russia has her good points.'

Galerkin was angry now, but he recognised his own vulnerability in this foreign land.

'I only have one asset left!' he shouted. 'And you call this a civilised democracy!'

'Yes, a sad state of affairs, I admit, and rest assured that your final asset will be left untouched. May I assume that this business was not of your own devising, that someone else was pulling the strings, and that, really, you are a true man of business?'

'Go on,' said Galerkin.

'Well,' continued Dawson, 'it may be beneficial to you, and to us, if you continue to finance your final asset on behalf of the puppet master, provided that I personally receive full details of such from time to time.'

'You are a man who takes great risks, Mister Anderson,' stated Galerkin, glancing towards the door.

'Would you like to be on board the five o'clock plane to Moscow, with your London coffers emptied, Mister Galerkin? Consider what I have said very carefully. Dual citizenship can be yours, a great honour, almost as good as that Premier League title, but such rewards have their price.'

With that, Dawson stood up and walked towards the door. Turning, he said:

'You have one day to think it over. If you decline my offer, it will not be me who comes through your door, next time.'

As Dawson left the palatial room, Galerkin shouted something in Russian to the two guards. They stood aside and let Dawson pass.

A minute later, the senior MI5 officer walked out of the block of flats into March sunshine. Sweat began to pour from his forehead as he hailed a taxi to return to Whitehall.

Back in his office, Galerkin sat alone, staring into space, digesting this turn of events. He thought, thought about all that he had here, here in London. The petty crook from St Petersburg was long gone. This Mister Anderson would have his way, but for him too there would be a price to pay. There was a knock at his door and a young man was ushered into the room by Galerkin's two security men.

The Russian looked up from his desk and said:

'Well, Anton, is everything in place as planned? If so, do it, and do it quickly!'

Anton Davidov nodded.

CHAPTER 22

For Anton Davidov this had become very personal. He and his three colleagues had all been handpicked from their university courses in Moscow to be trained to be destructive hackers at the highest level, to be able to disrupt encrypted websites and software vital to NATO defence systems. Yes, Galerkin had paid them extremely well for the past four years or so, but beneath that was an interdependence and a bond of achievement that had brought them closer and closer to each other, a band of brothers, even though their workstation locations had often been hundreds of miles apart. All that had come to an end, in Davidov's mind because of one man, a man who had outhacked the best of them, Jonathan Maxim. Nightjar's two games of chess against Spectrum had been enough to identify him. It was Maxim's use of a laptop tethered to an ordinary smartphone that had been the key. The security of the phone provider had been relatively weak and easy for Davidov to undermine. He would never have been able to achieve such a breakthrough via GCHQ's connection to his adversary.

Maxim's physical location within the UK had remained unknown, but not for long. This had needed some luck. Davidov trawled search engines for any mention of a Jonathan Maxim, but to no avail. Then, in desperation, he tried newspaper websites. His software found the name in an article on page four of a Sunday newspaper, dated the previous July. It included a brief press release from Skipton police, stating that they were searching for Mr Jonathan Maxim and Mrs Sally Henshaw in connection with the death of Mrs Elaine Law. To Davidov, it seemed most odd that his Jonathan Maxim, an expert hacker who he assumed was working for British security, should be the same Jonathan Maxim sought in relation to a killing in some out of the way place in northern England. Nevertheless, after consulting Galerkin, he contacted Viktor Barkov, best described as the oligarch's chief hitman, a man who terrified Davidov, and asked him politely to investigate.

When Davidov eventually arrived in London and informed Galerkin that not only did he know who had stolen the eighty-nine million dollars from the Isle of Man account, but that he now knew his probable location, his master had shown less interest than he had expected. The bank had made good the loss and Galerkin's thoughts had moved on to how he could retain his threatened billionaire lifestyle in London. His loyalty to Mother Russia had flagged, corrupted by decadence perhaps. The visit from the Home Office merely accelerated his thinking process. However, if he was to take on the role of a double agent, then Maxim's quick elimination could be most helpful, confirming his continued loyalty to his puppet masters. And so, he had given Davidov the go ahead.

Anton Davidov was no killer, but he wanted to be in on the kill. He wanted to see it happen in person, to exercise his revenge for the death of three friends. He had only met Viktor Barkov once, a man experienced in the art of assassination on behalf of the Russian state, a man who had been in Yorkshire now for seven days preparing the ground. As Davidov emerged from the King's Cross train at York station he was met with a look of steel. The two men left the station and walked a few hundred yards to a café on a picturesque bridge over the swift flowing Ouse. They sat with coffees at a table outside. Barkov was the first to speak.

'I am not happy with this situation, Davidov,' he said in a menacing tone. 'I do not know what the target looks like and neither do you. We only know his location and name, but little else. I have visited the location but could not get close. There were cameras everywhere. The target must be lured away from his hiding place. I have set something up to help us with this, but, more importantly, I am disturbed by your presence. You are an amateur in matters such as these, as is the target no doubt. You will only get in my way.'

Davidov started to sweat and stammered a little.

'Are you certain that this man is the man we seek?'

'Do you think that I am an idiot, Davidov? Yes, I am sure. I have discovered that British newspapers were silenced about the man's involvement in a killing at the same location last year, silenced by the British Secret Service. The man disappeared but, according to my source, has returned.'

'I am not here to get in your way, Viktor. I just wish to see for myself when my friends are avenged.'

'Spare me your sentimentality. Very well but do as I say at all times!'

They finished their coffees and then walked quickly to the nearest car park where Barkov had left his large black Range Rover. In the car Barkov made a phone call.

'Mister Davies? It's Vic, from the Standard. If you could set up your meeting with Jonathan Maxim and get back to me with full details, that would be excellent. Half of your fee will go into your account today, as agreed, the other half when we receive your interview transcript. The sooner the better, eh!'

Barkov's English accent was immaculate.

Only an hour later Sally Henshaw was called through to the bar telephone by her husband.

'It's that reporter Davies,' he shouted. 'Be careful.'

Sally picked up the phone. Davies was clearly in a hurry to see her brother to discuss her mother's death and what he called the goings on at Scargill Cottage. Sally was courteous and did as Tanner had told her. It was agreed that Davies would meet Jonathan at The Lion in Cray the following day at twelve o'clock.

After the call, Sally hurried to her bedroom and phoned Tanner. She told him exactly what the reporter had wanted.

'Don't worry, Mrs Henshaw,' said Tanner to reassure her, 'I'll be playing your brother and I'll be very careful what I say. If he gets too pushy, I may have to threaten him a bit. In the end, I can revert to a nasty MI5 man if needs be.'

'I think I should be there,' she said.

'Yes, I agree,' replied Tanner. 'It's what he'd expect. Remember, you will have to treat me just like you treat your brother. A smile would be a nice change.'

'Very funny, Mister Tanner.'

'Just a joke,' he added, 'but we will have to convince him, so he accepts that there is no real story, or I give him a harmless version that could make it into print. I'll work something out. I'll pick you up in the morning at eleven thirty.'

'Thank you, David,' she said, getting upset with herself.

She rushed downstairs to the kitchen where Tom was preparing sandwiches for hungry walkers and flung her arms around him. The big Yorkshireman embraced her and kissed her forehead.

'Don't worry, Sally,' he said, 'David Tanner knows what he's doing.'

CHAPTER 23

David Tanner was seated opposite Jonathan Maxim eating breakfast in the kitchen at Scargill Cottage. Tanner was having his usual full English whereas Jonathan was content to nibble away at two slices of buttered toast with several cups of tea. He had been told to be up early and had obliged. To Tanner's surprise this had included full makeup and the favourite long black dress trimmed with lace so reminiscent of his mother's taste in fashion.

'So, you've got it, Jonathan?' said Tanner. 'I'm going to pick your sister up at The Inn and then go to Cray and pretend to be you when we meet the annoyingly inquisitive reporter.'

'Would you like to borrow my dress?' quipped Maxim. 'Oh, no, I don't think you'd get in it. A bit on the large side.'

'This is no joking matter,' said Tanner sternly. 'I don't trust these arrangements. You'll be here on your own, so I suggest you keep a wary eye out with the security cameras while I'm gone.'

'You don't trust Davies? But we checked him out. He is who he claims to be.'

'Yes,' said Tanner, 'but it's all a bit too pat. It's over eight months since all hell broke loose up here and rumours have been circulating for ages. How come he's turned up now? And how come he knows you're Mrs Henshaw's brother, and that you're up here?'

'Yes, I've thought about that. All I could come up with was Fred Denby. Fred talks too much when he drinks too much.'

'Mmm, maybe. Anyway, keep a good look out and be prepared.'

Maxim laughed at this unintentional allusion to the boy scouts.

At 11.15 Tanner left Maxim to his own devices and set off for Buckden. Ten minutes later, as he turned the BMW into the pub car park, Sally Henshaw walked out of the back door. Behind her remained Tom, standing with his arms folded, mouthing 'good luck' and 'take care'. As she put on her seat belt Sally asked:

'What story are you going to tell Davies?'

Tanner didn't answer. He was still trying to work that one out for himself.

'Well?' she added.

'Just something simple. It depends what he asks,' came the less than helpful reply. 'Just remember, I'm Jonathan.'

The rest of the two-mile journey was in silence. Tanner came upon The Lion round a narrow tight bend and pulled off the road onto the loose-stone covered pull-in opposite. The building looked more like a farmhouse with an appropriate sign on its wall than an inviting pub-cum-hotel. As he walked quickly across the road, followed by Sally, he glanced back at the two other vehicles in the car park, one a large black Range Rover, the other an old red hatchback that had seen better days. He guessed which one of the two was owned by Davies.

The bar was as welcoming as ever, with its open fire and a smiling landlord.

'What would you like, Sal?' said Tanner as Davies approached with the offer of a handshake and a 'no, let me, Mister Maxim.'

'That's kind of you,' said Sally, 'I'll have a gin and tonic. Jonathan rarely drinks. He'll have sparkling water.'

Tanner smiled confidently and they all sat down at a small table near the fire. Tanner, as ever, glanced swiftly but carefully around the room. He got up and walked across to the wall opposite.

'Look, Sis,' he said, loudly, 'a smashing photo of the dale, the Triangle Walk I think.'

'Yes, it is, sir,' shouted Terry from behind the bar, then bringing over the drinks.

Tanner retook his seat. He'd seen enough. Two men were seated in the opposite corner, in semi-darkness, well away from the heat of the fire on this cold Spring morning, one slight and young, wearing an anorak, incongruous with the other, an older man, fit looking with a slight tell-tale bulge just below the right shoulder of his smart dark blue jacket.

'Left-handed and armed,' thought Tanner.

Davies began to ask Sally and Tanner questions. He seemed in a hurry and scribbled down their answers in a tatty notebook. Sally answered most of the early questions, in a truthful-sounding matter-of-fact way, every now and then smiling at 'her brother' and tapping him on the hand. Had it not been that Tanner was concentrating like hell, he might have found that pleasurable and amusing.

'So, Mister Maxim, you lived up at Scargill Cottage with your mother for four years or so, and your sister moved to the pub in Buckden when she got married. How did your mother die?'

The bluntness of the question from the reporter was meant to shock. Sally glanced nervously at Tanner who appeared unfazed.

'It was an awful accident, Mister Davies, my fault, but an accident.'

Tanner gave a deep sigh.

'Go on Mister Maxim.'

'I've always had this thing about rabbits. They eat everything in the garden. Anyway, I have an air pistol, quite a powerful one for what it is, and I shoot rabbits if they come anywhere near the cottage.'

Davies scribbled frantically.

'Go on,' he urged again.

'One morning I spotted a rabbit from the kitchen window. I opened the window and shot it. I put the pistol down and went outside to get the rabbit. My mother liked to cook rabbit. As I retrieved it, I heard the pistol go off and when I rushed back inside, I found my mother. Somehow, she had managed to shoot herself with it. In the eye. It was awful.'

'That seems a rather tall tale, Mister Maxim,' said Davies in disbelief.

'Yes, I know, that's why I panicked. I ran away. I know it was stupid of me. A day later I phoned Sally who calmed me down and came to get me.'

'Where from?' asked the reporter.

'Douglas, but by that time, police had put me on the news.'

'Indeed,' said Davies, sounding extremely sceptical.

'In the end,' said Sally, 'police realised that it had been a terrible accident. There was no evidence against Jonny, no evidence at all. He was distraught, poor thing. He went away for a few months to get over it all, and then came back to the cottage. He's very much a recluse now, aren't you, dear? All this has taken its toll.'

'Yes,' said Tanner, sighing again. 'I prefer my own company.'

Davies was unsure what to make of all this. It sounded nonsense, but he could check a few things out with his Skipton police contacts. He suddenly got out of his chair.

'Mind if I take a photograph of you both? The wronged brother and sister as you might say. I'd like to make some more enquiries of my own and then chat again if that's alright by you, up at Scargill Cottage if possible.'

Tanner stood up and took a step towards the reporter.

'No, Mister Davies,' he said in a tone meant to frighten, 'no photograph, and we'd prefer this to be your one and only interview. As for visiting me at the cottage, I think not. Rabbits haven't fared too well of late.'

Davies opened his mouth to argue the point but didn't. He turned and hurried out of the pub without another word. Tanner looked at Sally and said, in an overly loud voice:

'Time to take you home, Sis.'

As they left the pub and got in the BMW, they saw Davies' red hatchback race off. A few hundred yards down the road, Sally turned to Tanner.

'How do you think it went, David?'

'I don't think he believed a word. Would you?' he replied. 'Then again, he's got something to write, and his editor will get a call from one of ours tomorrow. I'm more concerned with the black car following us. Don't look back.'

As Tanner indicated left to pull in round the back of The Inn, he glanced in his mirror to see the Range Rover slowly continue on past. In the car park, Sally jumped out of the BMW and ran into Tom's arms. Tanner nodded across at him and turned the car around to set off back to Scargill Cottage. Less than a mile up the road he looked in his mirror and saw the black Range Rover following at a distance. A few hundred yards from Cray he stuck his foot down. He turned left and accelerated at high speed up the winding road, turning right after a mile, speeding between the conifer screen and down the drive to Scargill Cottage. He parked the car at the rear and rushed through the back door, and then into Maxim's room.

Jonathan was staring at the security camera screen, zooming in on the entrance to the driveway.

'There's movement in the trees, two men maybe,' he said. 'Who are they?'

'I don't know,' said Tanner. 'One just seems like a kid, the other I might have seen before, or maybe in a file somewhere. He's armed. They were watching us in the pub and then followed.'

'What do you think they think?' asked Maxim. 'Two of us in here or just one? Did they buy you as me?'

'Yes, I'm sure. Your sister was terrific, even smiled at me. But if I ever see that reporter again, he'll end up in hospital.'

After a minute or so, Jonathan stated: 'They've gone.'

'You stay here, and out of sight,' said Tanner. 'I'll check the perimeter.'

'Take care MI5.'

Fifteen minutes later Tanner was back in the cottage.

'All quiet out there and the Range Rover's gone. But they'll be back.'

'To kill you, not me,' quipped Maxim.

'To kill anyone they find,' said Tanner starkly.

'Who do you think they are? Are they anything to do with Donnelly?'

'I doubt that,' replied Tanner. 'My best guess is that they're Russian, sent by Galerkin. I need to talk to my boss.'

'I think I'll have a game of chess,' said Jonathan, wandering off to his room, apparently undisturbed by events.

Every ten minutes, for the following hour, Tanner tried Dawson's mobile and office numbers. Finally, he answered. Tanner told him, belatedly, about the reporter from the Post, and then the meeting in the pub, and the two men who had followed him back to the cottage.

'I think they're Russian, sir, Galerkin's men, here to kill Maxim.'

'Oh, dear, David, how tiresome. I visited Galerkin and was sure that I'd turned him. Where is honour amongst thieves, these days? Well, you will have to deal with the situation on your own, or just let Maxim take his chance as I said before. Galerkin is a big prize for us. I want him to keep running hackers but to feed us information. That way we can monitor them monitoring us.'

Tanner swore down the phone at his boss.

'Language, David. I do not understand why Galerkin has taken Maxim's involvement so personally. If you wish to protect him, then do so by all means but try not to get killed. The paperwork would be appalling!'

The call ended abruptly.

When Tanner walked somewhat disconsolately into Maxim's den, Jonathan was clapping himself, having just won his game. He was now ranked fourth on the chess ladder.

'My boss says that we're on our own. He can't understand why Galerkin might want you dead so badly. Anyway, apparently, MI5 is all friends with the Russian, even if he hates you. Why might that be?'

Jonathan just laughed.

'Well, Mister Tanner, you and I will have to clear the whole thing up for MI5 by ourselves. As you said, they will be back. I look forward to it. It has been overly quiet here of late. I assume that if I play my part, and it turns out well, then my freedom is assured?'

'How the hell should I know?' replied Tanner.

Jonathan frowned.

CHAPTER 24

When Viktor Barkov followed the speeding BMW up to Scargill Cottage he was already concerned at what he'd got himself into. He always obeyed his master, but this time could be different. He observed the cottage windows for several minutes through binoculars.

'Why don't we just go in there and kill him?' Davidov suggested with false bravery.

'No, my stupid friend,' was Barkov's reply.

After seeing what he needed to see, he pushed Davidov in the direction of the Range Rover and they left the scene quickly.

Barkov turned left at Cray and slowly proceeded to the top of Wharfedale on hairpin bends and winding roads strewn with wayward sheep. As Wensleydale came into view with its panoramic greenness, he came upon the small hotel he was seeking. He was still only nine miles from the cottage. Inside, he booked a large room with a smaller one through an adjoining door, family accommodation, as for parents and a small child. This amused Barkov.

'Tidy yourself up,' he ordered, oddly. 'We eat here tonight and do what is necessary tomorrow.'

Davidov was dismayed at this.

'I thought you were going to kill Maxim as he left that place with his sister, after the reporter had gone. That was the plan was it not?'

Barkov grabbed Davidov's anorak with his right hand and slapped him with his left.

'Never question what I do,' he said with venom. 'The man with Maxim's sister was not Maxim. He was a British Intelligence agent!'

Davidov opened his mouth but was unable to speak.

'You look scared my little cyberman. You should be!'

Barkov shoved him backwards against a wall, turned and went into the en suite bathroom, slamming the door behind him. Davidov walked towards the door to his tiny room. He needed a drink and, instead, hurried downstairs to the hotel bar.

Barkov sat in a chair next to his bed thinking while he drank coffee. No, the man was not Maxim. He remembered seeing him three or four years ago, bizarrely, a few days before the official opening of a state-of-the-art football stadium, attended by a member of the British royal family and, also, by Yevgeni Galerkin, the club chairman. The man had been one of a Special Branch team that had visited the stadium to assess event security. They were shown the physical measures put in place for the opening but, irritating to Galerkin, this particular officer had requested to see much more, including details of computer security at the club. Even then, it was clear that MI5 were taking a special interest in the Russian.

'Yevgeni, it's Barkov. We have a problem, sir.'

Barkov's words produced a sharp response from his boss when he answered the call.

'Has the target been eliminated?'

'No, sir. The man who we saw was not who we expected. He was an MI5 agent, obviously there to protect our target. How do you wish me to proceed?'

Galerkin thought quickly.

'This is bad, Viktor. The elimination of a hacker would be regarded as tit-for-tat as the British say, but, an MI5 man, that would not be tolerated. It would put my presence here in jeopardy. Things are at a very delicate stage. I suggest you abandon the project and return to London.'

'What about loose ends? Davidov? The reporter?' queried Barkov.

'The reporter knows nothing?'

'No, sir.'

'Then forget him. As for Davidov, he returns with you, Viktor.'

'He may be very unhappy about that, sir.'

'Use your own judgement.'

The call ended and Barkov lay down on his bed and slept for three hours. Davidov spent most of the time drinking vodka until the hotel barman suggested that he'd had enough. He returned to the room.

At six o'clock precisely, Barkov's heavy left fist knocked loudly on Davidov's door.

'Time for our meal, Davidov,' he shouted.

The pair ate an excellent roast dinner, followed by a cheese board, in total silence. Davidov had started to sober up but this was mitigated by a bottle of burgundy that Barkov had ordered for them both. As he finished his second glass, Barkov said, out of the blue:

'I have spoken to Yevgeni. The elimination is cancelled. We are to return to London tomorrow morning.'

'Just because of an MI5 agent!' came the angry reply.

'Yes,' said Barkov, 'he cannot be touched.'

'But Maxim can.'

'No, that is too risky. You must do as I say.'

'Are you scared, Viktor?'

'Do not be stupid. We leave in the morning, after breakfast.'

'Very well, Viktor,' said Davidov, in a way that managed to express acquiescence and resistance at the same time.

They returned to their room for the night.

Barkov awoke at around seven o'clock next morning. He shouted through to Davidov. There was no reply. He rushed to the door to the child's room and opened it. The room was empty. He turned quickly and grabbed his dark blue jacket. The car keys were gone. He stared down at his empty holster lying on a chair. His gun was gone too.

CHAPTER 25

As Anton Davidov drove slowly through the hairpin bends
and back down into Wharfedale, his mind churned with
anticipation and fear. He had stolen the Range Rover and
the gun. Barkov would be angry, he knew that, and he
himself was not a brave man, nor someone who had ever
killed, but he was consumed by the need to avenge the
deaths of his compatriots. This had been on the spur of the
moment, on waking early with anger in his veins. He
should have a plan but had none. Suddenly, The Lion came
into view and he made an instant decision. He braked
violently and swerved the car into the pull-in opposite the
pub. It was only seven thirty and all was silence around
him. He searched around in the car and found a map and a
bright blue scarf. His anorak was grey and reversible, with
a red lining. He got out of the car and closed the door
quietly. He turned the anorak inside out and put it on, with
the scarf half-covering the lower part of his face.

'Today I am a hiker, and I look different to when I was last
here,' he said out loud, trying to give himself confidence.

He removed the small snub-nosed revolver from his pocket
and checked it. He breathed in deeply as he counted the six
bullets, nerves, for the moment, getting the better of him.
He did not think to look in the boot of the Range Rover

where he would have found Barkov's high-powered rifle, admittedly disassembled, hidden inside a briefcase.

He had decided to walk up to the cottage, with no car to giveaway his arrival or possible intention. He strode off quickly and turned right around the bend, passing the few houses that constituted Cray. He looked ahead at the steep winding climb. He slowed and it wasn't until Hubberholme church sounded eight o'clock that he turned right into the entrance to Scargill Cottage driveway. He must be confident now. He was an early morning walker finding his way.

He walked casually and slowly down the centre of the drive, pulling the map out of his left-hand pocket, feigning to study it more than once.

In his den, Jonathan Maxim was sat at his laptop, but with bright blue eyes fixed on the security screen to his left, watching a man approaching the cottage, a man he did not recognise, but a man looking like a lost soul who, like many before him, had taken a wrong turn on the Triangle Walk. Yet, Jonathan remembered the last time this had happened, when Peter Wilson, a retired MI5 officer, had met his death. Jonathan studied the man carefully and then, happy with what he saw, turned back to his laptop.

'Tanner can deal with him,' he said to himself.

Davidov walked through the garden gate and down the narrow path to the front door. He knocked twice, and then a third time more loudly, and took three steps backwards. David Tanner was in the front room, checking emails and drinking coffee. He was shocked by the sudden knock at the door. Maxim was supposed to be watching out for anyone.

'Jonathan,' he shouted, 'who's at the door? Is it your sister?'

'No, just some walker, lost I think,' came the casual reply.

'You think!' shouted Tanner. 'Idiot!'

Tanner got off the sofa and walked cautiously towards the front door, tapping his holster as he went. He took out his pistol and, caressing it in his right hand, slowly opened the front door with his left. Anton Davidov was standing only ten feet away, with his right arm stretched out in front of him, revolver in hand, a nervous finger touching the trigger. Tanner recognised him immediately. Size, shape, eyes, nose, he had been trained to observe and to remember. He knew he had no time to slam the door and took a step forwards, holding up his left hand in a defensive gesture, keeping his right perfectly still by his side.

'Where is Maxim?' said the Russian.

'I am Maxim,' replied Tanner. 'You saw me in the pub yesterday. I was with my sister.'

'You lie. You are a British agent. Where is Maxim? Tell me or I shall kill you.'

'He is no longer here. He's back in London.'

'I do not believe you. If he was gone, then you would be too.'

At that moment, Jonathan Maxim emerged from the doorway behind Tanner, a red lipstick smile on his face, in the long black dress and high heels. Davidov's pistol barrel shifted its intent momentarily from Tanner to Maxim and then back again. Tanner's right hand still did not move.

Davidov stared at Jonathan, his brain confused by mixed messages his eyes were giving him.

'Who are you?' he shouted at the pretty face in the black dress.

'I am David's girlfriend,' was the reply. 'I am here on holiday.'

Tanner still did not move.

'What nonsense is this!' shouted Davidov. 'Who are you? Answer or I kill you both. And where is Maxim!'

Davidov's anger was overtaking him now and his arm began to shake.

'Why, don't you recognise me?' said Jonathan. 'Do you play chess?'

Davidov's eyes stared at the pretty face and, suddenly, his brain knew.

Tanner adjusted the pistol in his right hand but, in that same instant, Davidov shifted his aim to Tanner's head. As his brain gave his hand the signal to pull the trigger, Maxim pulled a knife from his left sleeve and the full extent of the stiletto blade hurtled into Davidov's heart. The revolver fell from his hand and he crumpled to the ground.

Jonathan stared down at the dead body lying at his feet. He slowly withdrew the knife and cleaned the blade theatrically by wiping it several times across the red anorak.

'Anton Davidov, I presume,' said Jonathan, turning his head to smile at Tanner. 'Not as good a hacker as me, not as good a chess player as me, and not as fast as me.'

'And not as good a killer as you,' added Tanner, sitting on the ground next to the body and shaking his head. He knew that Davidov was no assassin, just an avenging hacker out of his depth.

They heard a car engine start up beyond the end of the drive and a black Range Rover approached at a crawl down the driveway. It stopped about fifty yards from them. Tanner got to his feet to see the other man that he had seen in The Lion the previous day, the one he'd half-recognised, emerging from the car, holding both hands aloft.

'This is over,' shouted Barkov. 'I will do you no harm, but I shall take Davidov with me.'

'What is your name,' shouted Tanner.

'Viktor Barkov,' came the reply. 'And yours?'

'David Tanner.'

'I have seen you before.'

'And I you,' said Tanner.

'Who is the girl? She is excellent with a knife.'

Tanner nodded.

'Her name doesn't matter. You wouldn't know her.'

Jonathan blew Barkov a kiss, turned and walked back into the cottage.

Barkov and Tanner carried the body of Anton Davidov to the Range Rover and placed it in the boot. Barkov covered the body with a sheet and muttered a prayer in Russian. He turned to Tanner and said:

'I hope that we do not meet again, Mister Tanner. It would be very bad for one of us, you I think.'

Tanner looked in the car and saw a high-powered rifle with telescopic sights lying on the back seat. He backed away and stood still in the middle of the driveway until the car was out of sight. He stared upwards at the heavens and then tapped his holster three times. When he walked back into the cottage and went through to the den, he found Jonathan Maxim sat at his laptop, playing chess.

CHAPTER 26

As Viktor Barkov sped down the M1 at a constant speed of eighty miles an hour he replayed the events of the day in his mind. The Range Rover was set on cruise control and, with diplomatic immunity, there was no fear at being stopped by an overzealous police officer.

Early that morning, when he had discovered that Davidov and the car were gone, he'd found the hotel owner and spent tortuous minutes persuading him that he needed to get to Cray, urgently, much to the man's puzzlement. In the end, five twenty-pound notes had done the trick. With a cheery wave the Yorkshireman had at last dropped the Russian off outside The Lion after crawling his way from the hotel over into Wharfedale. Using his spare car keys, Barkov quickly retrieved the rifle in the boot of the Range Rover and reassembled it. He then set off at speed through Cray, up the long winding climb. As the entrance to Scargill Cottage came into view he slowed the Range Rover, coming to a halt only thirty yards from the driveway. Carrying the rifle in both hands he jogged from the car and positioned himself out of sight within the conifers and observed from the end of the drive.

By that time Anton Davidov was standing outside the cottage, arm outstretched, revolver in hand, threatening the life of the British Intelligence officer who Barkov had been ordered not to harm. Barkov balanced his rifle on a small branch of the tree he was hiding next to and stared through the telescopic sight. His aim focused on the back of Davidov's head and he was about to pull the trigger when an attractive young woman appeared next to the man he was about to save. He hesitated. What happened next, he could hardly fathom. The girl seemed merely to touch the left sleeve of her black dress and then a knife flashed through the morning sunlight and Davidov dropped to the ground. He had never seen such hand speed in all his years as a professional assassin.

As Barkov continued his journey down the motorway, he wondered who the girl was, and asked himself 'where was Maxim?' The hacker was probably in the cottage, hiding, was his conclusion. As for the girl? Clearly a professional like himself. Davidov had not only been stupid and impetuous, but unlucky too, perhaps.

After a five-hour drive from the diminutive village of Cray to London, Barkov finally arrived at Kensington Palace Gardens and the Embassy. He had rung ahead to say that he had a repatriation problem. At midnight, the body of Anton Davidov was winging its way back to Mother Russia in what may best be described as an oversized diplomatic bag.

After a very much needed evening dinner and a bottle of the best French red wine that the Embassy could muster, Barkov returned to his private room and consulted his laptop. There was an encrypted message from Moscow. He decrypted it using the requisite password and read it several times. He then replied to the message by querying its implication. The response was immediate and threatening. Barkov instantly acquiesced and made ready for the following morning and his return journey to Moscow.

In the morning Barkov's breakfast was a single black coffee. He rang Yevgeni Galerkin and told him, to the billionaire's surprise, that he had been ordered to return to Russia. Galerkin invited him for a final vodka. They had been friends, if the relationship between a master and an assassin can imply such, for over five years now. Barkov carried a single suitcase down to the Embassy foyer and met his driver who took him first to Galerkin's Mayfair apartment block.

'I shall only be five minutes,' said Barkov as he got out of the white Mercedes.

He walked into the building and was met with a smile from the usual receptionist and looks of respect and fear from the two security guards. Barkov was shown into Galerkin's private lift and emerged on the top floor to be greeted by a nod from a third guard. Galerkin's office door was already half open and Barkov entered to see his master pouring two large glasses of vodka and then setting them down on the marble desktop. The two men sat opposite each other.

'I won't ask what happened Viktor, but it is a pity about Davidov. I assume he died because he insisted on killing their hacker and their MI5 man.'

'Yes, Yevgeni,' replied Barkov.

The two men did not dwell on the matter but merely exchanged pleasantries for a few minutes. Barkov then stood up and, taking his glass in his left hand, raised it and said:

'To you Yevgeni and to a bright future here in London.'

'To you Viktor and to a bright future in Moscow.'

They both laughed and emptied their glasses in one gulp.

Barkov held out his right hand, reciprocated by his master, and clasped it in a final handshake, smiling.

The needle point pierced the flesh but a quarter of an inch. Galerkin stared at his friend in horror and collapsed to the floor, his body convulsing for only a few seconds before adopting a rigid pose with eyes wide open staring into eternity.

Barkov carefully removed the ring from his right middle finger and replaced it in a small metal box in his jacket pocket. He left the room quickly and nodded at the guard outside.

Two hours later Viktor Barkov flew out of Heathrow back to his true masters.

Two days later there was a headline on the back page of a national UK newspaper, alongside a photograph of Yevgeni Galerkin in the stands of his own football club stadium. The headline read:

'Galerkin dead of heart attack.'

CHAPTER 27

When Dawson was informed by Tanner that the only remaining hacker in Galerkin's team, Anton Davidov, the one that he had intended to continue hacking under the watchful eye of MI5, had been killed by Jonathan Maxim in order to save Tanner's own life, he was not, to use his own words, a happy bunny. When, two days later, he received the news that his intended double agent, Yevgeni Galerkin, had died of a spurious heart attack, his anger knew no bounds and he summoned David Tanner to London for a clear the air discussion.

Tanner received the summons at seven o'clock in the morning. He rang Sally Henshaw and suggested that she and Tom come up to Scargill Cottage to be with Jonathan for a while. He didn't really believe that he needed looking after, but his sister's presence was a calming influence. Tanner's view was that Maxim was no longer in imminent danger. Donnelly was dead. Davidov was dead. Galerkin was dead.

At two o'clock that afternoon Tanner knocked and entered his boss's office, to find Tony Masters, his CIA contact, listening to a smiling Dawson talking in a very animated fashion.

'Welcome, David,' said Dawson. 'Since we talked on the phone this morning, our American cousins have been in touch. I've been saying to Tony, you know each other of course, how well things have turned out.'

His boss smiled at them both in a way that only he could when lying through his teeth. Tanner's mouth opened but a hand gesture from Dawson closed it immediately.

Tony turned to Tanner and smiled, with a 'yes, good job.'

'Perhaps you'd care to explain to David the view from across the pond?' said Dawson.

'Sure,' replied Tony. 'Well, after our last King's Cross coffee the Agency looked into disposing of the oligarch, but his security was very tight, and the elimination was proving to be more difficult than we anticipated. But now, there is no Galerkin and you even managed to get rid of the last of the guys who hacked into our Defense sites. Good outcome, David.'

Tapping Tanner on the shoulder, Masters turned to the more senior British Secret Service officer and nodded.

'Thanks for the debrief, Mister Dawson.'

He turned away, winked at Tanner, and left the office.

Tanner opened his mouth to speak.

'Don't, David,' said Dawson, raising his right hand, 'what a bloody shambles! Sit down.'

For the following hour, the two of them discussed the events at Scargill Cottage since Jonathan Maxim had been taken back there at the start of January. Periodically, Dawson shook his head in disbelief.

'To summarise, you're telling me that, in your view, it is we and not Maxim who are responsible for this fiasco, on the basis that he was working for us and GCHQ.'

'Yes, sir,' said Tanner. 'Maxim did everything we asked of him, no more, no less. He found four highly dangerous hackers. All are dead. He identified Galerkin as the man behind them, although, in truth, we know that he was a Moscow stooge living the high life over here. Galerkin is dead, not your preferred outcome, I know, but probably killed by Barkov, certainly not us. That may be your fault, sir, assuming Moscow got wind of your visit to the oligarch. You're probably in their files.'

'Thank you, David! So, the Galerkin business is closed. A pity, but the Americans are pleased. I still don't understand why Galerkin put so much effort into trying to kill Maxim. And allowing Davidov's involvement, why take such a risk?'

'I think Davidov was provoked by Maxim and that he wanted revenge, although it was MI6 who eliminated the rest of the hacker team. As for Galerkin's persistence, that too puzzles me. Never know now, sir.'

'And what about Donnelly? I just about buy him wishing to kill Michael Maxim, assuming that he didn't know that he was dead, of course, but who do you think killed Donnelly?'

'My best guess is Barkov. We know that he must have been in the area for some time and I think it was happenstance. Donnelly and Barkov turned up at Scargill Cottage on the same night and one of them had to be the loser.'

'And what about the broken-off knife blade? Odd, don't you think?'

'Yes, but it did make the killing look amateurish at first sight.'

'Perhaps, David. That would tidy everything, but it doesn't sit well with me. I don't feel comfortable with it, a gut feeling as you'd say.'

Tanner nodded, although it was a phrase he never used.

'What are we going to do with Jonathan Maxim, sir? His six months will be up soon, and GCHQ seem to be using him less and less.'

'Oh, God knows!' exclaimed Dawson, 'He should probably be certified and put back in the clinic or some out of the way asylum. I think he requires debriefing and assessment again. What is your view?'

'I don't think we'd learn anything new. Maxim is excellent at hiding information in his head. You only get a partial view. Personally, I would leave him where he is and monitor him. He appears to be stable so long as he can see his sister. We think of him as a killer, but, if he hadn't killed Davidov, I wouldn't be standing here, sir, and your paperwork would have gone through the roof.'

'OK, David. I'll put it to the committee and seek advice from the clinic. I suppose his talents could still be useful to us in the future. Let's give it a month or so and then reassess.'

'Thank you, sir.'

Their meeting ended and Tanner rushed out of the Whitehall building to get a taxi to King's Cross. Overall, he knew that he'd got lucky, thanks to the Americans. He was pleased that he'd rung Tony that morning before getting the train south.

CHAPTER 28

Over the following days Jonathan Maxim became more and more reflective about recent events, seeking to rationalise his own involvement. Months before he had been ecstatic at escaping the clinic and returning to Scargill Cottage, with Sally nearby to help him through any darkness that invaded his mind. The work for GCHQ had been stimulating for a while, but his games with Galerkin and Davidov, that at first had amused him, had gone badly wrong. Oh yes, he had proved his usefulness to MI5 by identifying the Russian's team, but he hadn't meant for the hackers to die. They had minds and abilities like his own. It hadn't seemed to matter at first. The three eliminated by MI6 were in countries far away. But Davidov's death was by Jonathan's own hand, outside his own door, and Davidov played chess with him and had proved that his expertise was just as good as his own by finding out who he was and where he was. Maybe Davidov was even better than Jonathan himself. And now, even Galerkin was dead. What was the point of having all that money, the Russian's money, if he was dead? There was none. No point at all! Jonathan's mind was full of confusion.

'I think I have something important to tell you,' said Maxim to David Tanner as they both sat down in the kitchen one evening to eat a meal prepared by Sally. She looked at her brother, worried by what words might come out of his mouth.

'Really?' said Tanner, uninterested.

'Yes, I'm not happy about all this. Anton Davidov was a friend of mine and you made me kill him. He played chess with me.'

'Davidov came here to kill you, not me, Jonathan. You are mis-thinking.'

'Why would he want to kill me? We played chess.'

Tanner was staggered by such sentiments.

'You found Davidov and his colleagues for MI6. Their deaths were as a direct result of your actions, Jonathan. Davidov came here for revenge.'

'No,' said Maxim, 'he was sent by Galerkin to get the money back, that's all. If I'd given him the money, we could still have been friends.'

Sally grabbed hold of her brother's left hand to comfort him. Jonathan was starting to cry. Tanner spoke slowly, with precision.

'What money, Jonathan? Tell me about the money. What have you done?'

Maxim's face changed instantly. Tears were replaced by a boyish grin.

'Oh, it's no fun now, Mister Tanner. I don't need the money, you see. I can make money any time, just ask Sal. I used to play on the FTSE, but Sal stopped me after all the fuss when you took my money away. So, I thought I'd get it back, from Galerkin. After all, he had billions, so I took some, from the account he used to pay his hackers, for fun really. I think it must have annoyed him, really annoyed him, but why, when you have billions, why Mister Tanner? I was going to give it back to him sometime, after the game was over, but he's dead. No fun now.'

'How much did you take, Jonny?' asked Sally.

Jonathan winked a smile at his sister and whispered loudly.

'Eighty-nine million dollars.'

David Tanner was about to swear but then began to laugh uncontrollably. Jonathan looked at him with curiosity and then joined in. Sally rose to her feet.

'You're like two juvenile hyenas!' she shouted, but then burst out laughing, just the same.

Tanner suddenly leapt out of his chair and ran over to the fridge, returning with a bottle of white wine. He poured two glasses hurriedly, spilling a substantial amount over the table. He handed Sally a glass and raised his own.

'To Jonathan Maxim. Nostrovia!'

Jonathan's face froze at the repetition of his own toast weeks before, while Sally sank her glass, nervous of what might happen next.

'What are you going to do?' she asked almost pleadingly of Tanner. 'Don't send Jonny back. He needs to be with me.'

There was no bravado in Jonathan's face any more, no boyishness, just fear. He'd been back in Scargill Cottage for months now and, despite everything that had gone wrong, he knew he could cope if he had familiarity around him, and his sister. But he also knew that confinement, to be back in the clinic or worse, would be the end of him.

The brother and sister, so close since the day they were born, only minutes apart, studied the reaction of the MI5 officer, waiting for his judgement on their future.

'I will do my best for you, Jonathan,' he said. 'I don't want you to go back to the clinic, but you can never be free.'

'I don't mind, Mister Tanner, not really. Everything's hard for me, it always has been. I've always needed help, from father or mother or Sal, or even from Fred. I'll do whatever you want if I can stay here.'

Tanner was shocked by his own emotional response to this man, or perhaps this boy, who he'd thought of as dangerous, a man who could kill but who now was someone who had saved the MI5 officer from a Russian hacker's bullet. He nodded at the two siblings, poured himself another glass of wine and went through to the front room to sit on his own and think.

'What will happen now, Sal?' asked Jonathan.

'I think everything's fine, Jonny. Everything's fine.'

She ruffled her brother's hair and smiled.

'Make me a pot of tea, Sal, please. I'd like to go to my room.'

'You do that,' she replied and kissed him on the forehead.

CHAPTER 29

So, Jonathan Maxim had purloined eighty-nine million from a Russian oligarch's account on the Isle of Man, as a game, for fun, to prove to himself that he could, and to get back the money that MI5 had stolen from him. Was it pounds or dollars? Tanner could not recall as his train hurtled southwards. He'd had a couple of days to think over what he was going to say to his boss and what he felt about what should happen to Jonathan, but, at two o'clock, when he entered the conference room adjacent to Dawson's office, he was met by three men standing, not one, and none looked welcoming. His boss introduced Tanner to the other two men. One was rather dapper, with loud shirt and bow tie, whilst the other looked a little unkempt in a much older and tired looking suit.

'Gentlemen, this is David Tanner, the officer in charge of Jonathan Maxim. David, this is Doctor Taggart from GCHQ, and this is Detective Superintendent Fuller from the Metropolitan Police, who you may have met.'

'No, sir,' said Tanner, nodding at both men.

'When you emailed me to say that you had something important to discuss regarding Galerkin's financing of the Russian hacking team, I had just received information from GCHQ and DS Fuller who is liaising with authorities on the Isle of Man.'

'You see,' interrupted Fuller, 'since Yevgeni Galerkin met recently with an untimely death, it has been necessary to investigate his estate and assets very speedily, to ensure that his investments legitimately remain in the UK. During this investigation something came to light regarding Galerkin's account with Chamberland Asset Bank.'

'You mean it disappeared,' said Tanner, much to Dawson's obvious annoyance.

'You know about this?' asked the man from GCHQ.

Tanner nodded. Taggart continued.

'Yes, Mister Tanner, eighty-nine million dollars disappeared in a puff of smoke, with no trace of who took it or where it went. Quite remarkable. CAB were obliged to make good Galerkin's loss but now, well, they'd quite like their money back.'

'And you think I know where it is? And that I can get it back for you?' said Tanner with more than a glimmer of a smile. 'No doubt someone far cleverer than I am managed to open the safe and escape with the loot.'

'Stop pratting about, David,' shouted Dawson. 'Did Jonathan Maxim do this? Apparently, GCHQ believe that he did because they can't find out how the hell it could have happened and they can't trace where the money is, even after, so they tell me, interrogating every bank on the UK mainland and on the Isle of Man!'

Tanner saw three angry faces. His humour had not been appreciated.

'Let us suppose that someone did steal the money, after identifying the whereabouts of a team of cyber specialists, run by Galerkin, who had undermined UK and US defence, something vital to us all, and that he mistakenly did it for a game, putting his own life in danger, and my own, in fact, and that he eliminated the last of the team in order to save the life of an MI5 officer. What would you do now with such a thief?'

Fuller mouthed abuse at Tanner but was restrained by Dawson.

'My decision,' said Dawson, 'would be that you, David, are best placed to decide what is to be done with him. By now, you know him best, I believe, but be aware that his future conduct would be deemed your responsibility if anything untoward should happen.'

David Tanner said nothing for ten seconds or more, and then nodded at his superior. He reached inside his jacket pocket and removed a single piece of paper.

'Well, sir, I cannot give you proof that Jonathan Maxim was involved in any of this, but I do have details of where the eighty-nine million dollars now reside.'

'Well man, where is it?' came the immediate question from his superior.

Tanner handed the piece of paper to Dawson who stifled a guffaw. He turned to Taggart and Fuller.

'Gentlemen,' he said with great seriousness, 'I have here an account number, an account holder and the name of a bank. Apparently, the eighty-nine million dollars that you seek has magically returned to Chamberland Asset Bank and is held in an account owned by a Mister Robin Hood.'

He handed the piece of paper to Fuller who immediately left the room, swearing at Tanner as he did so.

Taggart turned to Dawson.

'I thought that we had learned all Maxim's tricks but somehow I think we've only just started. Perhaps we shall never be able to do what he does. He is a one-off. I suggest that we keep him in our employ. I leave it to you and MI5 to sort out the details.'

He then turned to Tanner.

'Well done, Mister Tanner, I think. Look after the boy.'

At that, he brushed past him and was gone.

Tanner examined the face of his boss with fingers crossed. Dawson sat down at the conference table, leant back in his chair, and folded his arms.

'I can't help but feel that you're a lucky bugger, David.'

Tanner breathed a sigh of relief and sat down opposite his superior.

'What about Maxim, sir?'

'Well, after what GCHQ has just suggested, I think we stick with what I said earlier. It's your call, David, but GCHQ want him and we both know that he can't function if we take him away from his sister.'

'What about me, sir?'

'What about you, David? Tidy up in Yorkshire and then get back to London where you belong. We can't have you going native living in the Dales, can we?'

'No, sir,' said Tanner.

CHAPTER 30

Jonathan Maxim had agreed to return Yevgeni Galerkin's money to Chamberland Asset Bank, as he put it, 'as a good will gesture, with a touch of humour', desperately hoping that he would be able to stay in Wharfedale. Despite this, when summoned to London, Tanner was certain that Maxim would shortly be forced to pack his bags and be returned to confinement, probably at the clinic on the Isle of Man. He had been saved by his own brilliance. GCHQ still had need of him, a need now expected to be on a permanent basis.

Possibly due to the interminable desire for due process in the British Civil Service, a few days after Tanner's return to Scargill Cottage, Maxim received a contract of employment. He provided an online signature of agreement without even reading it. The previous day, down at The Inn, David Tanner had spent three hours going through every detail with the Henshaws so that they understood all implications, both for Jonathan and for themselves.

After Jonathan agreed to his terms of employment, David Tanner explained the gist of it, with Sally and Tom Henshaw both present, then reading directly from an email he'd been sent via Dawson.

'Jonathan Maxim is to be in the permanent employ of GCHQ and situated at Scargill Cottage, near Cray in

Wharfedale, Yorkshire, at a rate of pay commensurate with his Civil Service grade, and to be officially under the care of his next of kin, Mrs Sally Henshaw, regarding his health and wellbeing, with his immediate superior, located at GCHQ, being Doctor Julian Hart, responsible for Special Projects Assignments. Overall, David Tanner, MI5 Officer, will be responsible for his conduct. There is to be no restriction on his movement, which continues to be monitored. This arrangement will be reappraised on an annual basis.'

'Do you understand what this means for you, Jonathan?' asked Tanner.

'Yes, I officially work for GCHQ now. I have a job here, looked after by my sister, and every now and then you'll turn up to annoy me.'

Jonathan smiled a normal broad smile and received a hug from Sally. Tom rather formally shook his hand.

'That's about right,' said Tanner. 'From now on everything you do is official government work, instigated by GCHQ and is classified. Secret, Jonathan. And for God's sake stay out of mischief. All gizmos remain in place here, security cameras etcetera, but I am sure that you are no longer in danger. You can lead what you regard as a normal life. You will see me probably about once a month, although I will also keep in touch online. The GPS chip must remain in place, but only because we need to know where you are at all times. Is that clear?'

'Yes, Mister Tanner. I can ride my quadbike and go to the shops and buy new clothes and see Fred and Tom and Sally. And play chess and maybe make a little profit with investments.'

He grinned his boyish grin and Tanner shook his head.

'If you want to make extra money, try the horses with Fred Denby. He needs your help too.'

To Maxim's surprise, Tanner held out his right hand. The man in the long black dress with white lace trim, bobbed black hair, and immaculately made up, with bright red lipstick and nail polish, did likewise and they shook hands, for the first time accepting each other for what they were.

Tanner had already placed his baggage in the BMW. He hated long goodbyes, even temporary ones, and merely wished them all good luck before walking out of Scargill Cottage. A minute later his car disappeared from view, as it turned left at the end of the driveway to head off down to Cray and, eventually, London and MI5 headquarters.

CHAPTER 31

It was a bright Saturday morning at the end of May.
Jonathan Maxim was alone in Scargill Cottage, but he
wasn't lonely. He enjoyed his own company, so long as he
had a plan for his day. He liked structure and now he had
one. He worked for GCHQ and was paid a salary. For the
first time ever, he felt accepted by the world in which he
lived. No, he wasn't free as other men are free, but he
didn't want such freedom. His world might be small but,
within its confines, he could do what he was good at, enjoy
what he enjoyed, and only be with the people he wanted to
be with.

That morning he dressed in blue jeans and black tea shirt,
with no makeup and, after tea and toast, rushed out of the
back door to his quadbike. It was caked in mud from
months before. A power hose and a bucket of soapy water
soon made it look immaculate. He had not been past the
exit to the drive for months but today he would have a ride
out. He drove slowly round to the front of the cottage and
positioned the quadbike on the drive facing the conifers
two hundred yards off. He revved the engine and slipped
the clutch, the quadbike powering forwards down the drive.
As he reached the exit he slammed on the brakes and
turned the handlebars. The grip of the tractor-like tyres held
the road and he was out, out onto the lane that led up to
Scargill Farm. After only a few hundred yards, he slowed

and turned left down a short narrow track to meet a section of the Triangle Walk. He braked to a halt and got off the quadbike. He was at the top of the scar, the crags that linked the path from Hubberholme to the road down to Cray. Set out below him was the vista he loved, Wharfedale stretching out for miles, with the two green sides of the valley converging in the distance on the River Wharfe. To the left, some two miles off, he could easily make out the whitewashed walls of The Inn, down in Buckden, where Sally and Tom would be getting ready to open the pub. No, he would never be far from his sister, and that is how it must be.

Jonathan stood there for minutes, taking in the view from the edge of his world, before hearing walkers coming around the crags, jabbering away to each other. He got back on the quadbike and retraced his route over a small rise back to the lane leading to Fred Denby's. He sauntered along wondering how Fred would be. He hadn't seen him for ages and no doubt rumours would be circulating yet again about the happenings at Scargill Cottage. He went through the open farm gates and came to a halt next to the familiar green Rover just beyond the old stone farmhouse, greeted by much barking of two familiar border collies. He switched off the quadbike.

'You in there Fred?' he shouted. 'Fancy a walk out?'

The green farmhouse door creaked open to reveal a smiling sixty-year-old overweight farmer.

185

'Hello, Jon my boy, good to see you at long last. Rumour was that you'd been taken away by the authorities, whoever they are. Had a bit of trouble?'

'A bit,' replied Jonathan, pleased at his reception.

Jonathan had known Fred for almost six years. It had started as a monetary arrangement, whereby the farmer was paid cash every month to deter troublesome walkers, or any other errant tourists, from coming anywhere near Scargill Cottage. Barking dogs, loud expletives, fist waving, Keep Out signs and a few firings of his twelve-bore had done the trick, and provided Fred with a nice income to fund his betting. Since his wife had died, ten years before, Fred's attention to the farm had wilted, although he still made money from bullocks and sheep. Originally, there had been four Maxims hiding away at Scargill Cottage. Michael Maxim had met his demise some five years ago and Sally had moved out a year later when she married Tom. After that Jonathan had been there with his mother, each with an uncanny resemblance to the other, especially when, as he often did, Jonathan dressed in his mother's clothes. Over the years Jonathan had come to regard Fred as a friend, not just a helpful and necessary acquaintance. The Yorkshire farmer, conservative to his soul, seemed to take no notice of Jonathan's unusual dress code, apart, perhaps, from an occasional wry smile. This odd pairing had got on famously, especially when enjoying walking the fields and having a shot or two at rabbits or pigeons or ravenous rooks. Even Fred's passion for horseracing and betting was a common enjoyment. Many a time Jonathan had sat on a Saturday afternoon with Fred explaining how the odds were rigged against the punter and offering advice, rarely taken by the farmer.

'I got my two-two back,' said the farmer with a grin. 'A young policeman, Craven was his name, turned up. Swore blind nobody had been shot with it. And then he gave me a formal warning about not having a licence. Bloody cheek!'

Jonathan laughed while Fred went back into the house and emerged carrying the two-two, with a pocketful of bullets.

'I'll lock the dogs up, then we can have a few pops,' said Fred. 'You probably need the practice.'

There was irony in his voice. He had seen Maxim's expertise many times before.

They played their game for the next hour or so. Fred would genuinely attempt to shoot a rabbit in flight, and invariably miss, while Jonathan would pick one off and then insist that it was luck.

'It's a damn sight easier with my twelve-bore,' said Fred as they walked back to the farmhouse.

Fred rambled on, while Jonathan remained quiet. He was enjoying the farmer's company. He was ordinary, and, although he would never admit to thinking it, he was like a normal father that he had never had.

As the two men went through the farmhouse front door, Fred casually leant the rifle against the hallway wall next to an old pair of wellington boots and led Jonathan through to his front room, a poorly lit den for a farmer who lived alone, not redecorated for some thirty years now, and rarely tidied these days.

'Switch the television on and sit yourself down, Jon. Put it on the racing channel. There's racing at York today and I've had a few bets. I'll go make us a cup of tea and get some biscuits.'

With that, Fred left the front room and went into the farmhouse kitchen. Like the rest of the house, it had seen better days, but those were days when Fred's wife had ruled the roost and kept everything ship shape. Now, everywhere seemed sad. It had been like that ever since Mrs Denby had been killed absentmindedly stepping out into the road one afternoon in Skipton while doing her weekly shop.

Nevertheless, Fred did have the horses, and he returned to Jonathan with a tray and an enthusiastic smile. For the following two hours he sat staring at the television, with the Racing Post set out before him on the front room table, every now and then making marks on the race cards in biro, and consulting Jonathan about the bets he was making using his mobile phone. Jonathan made suggestions primarily based on odds and, after five races, to Fred's huge pleasure, he was up to the tune of sixty-eight quid.

When the racing finished Fred offered his guest an apple to eat which was gratefully accepted.

'I'm having one myself,' said Fred. 'I usually have one after a win.'

'I know,' said Jonathan. 'You always have an apple if you win. It's a superstition of yours. You told me. If you have an apple then it means that you'll win again next time, that's what you said. It doesn't necessarily happen though, Fred, does it?'

'Sometimes it does,' replied the farmer with a smile.

'That's called chance,' said his friend.

Fred disappeared into the kitchen and reappeared with two large green apples and a sharp kitchen knife. He tossed an apple to Jonathan and then sat back down at the table. As Jonathan crunched his teeth into his apple, Fred began doing what he always did, which was to carefully cut thin slices of apple off and deposit them one by one into his mouth. He'd eaten apples this way for fifty years or more, mimicking his father's technique ever since he was a boy.

Jonathan stared across at the farmer, the apple, and the kitchen knife. When light dawned on him it did so in an instant and with certainty.

'You always eat your apple like that, Fred, without biting on it.'

'Yes,' replied the farmer, 'just like my Dad.'

'But you never use a kitchen knife.'

Maxim's tone was measured.

'Sometimes I do,' replied Denby, nervously.

'No, you don't, Fred. You always use an old knife you pull out of your jacket pocket. A flick knife from memory, probably the very one that your father used to use.'

The farmer stared at Maxim, unable to speak.

'Where is the knife, Fred?'

'Must have mislaid it, Jon, my boy,' he replied, desperately trying to smile but failing.

'You still have the handle, don't you, Fred? You'll have kept that. It was your father's. But the blade, Fred, you don't have that anymore, do you? And we both know where it is. It's in the chest of an American!'

The farmer put his head in his hands and stared down at the floor.

'God forgive me, Jon, I never meant to kill him, but it was him or me, and he was a big bloke, and he had a gun. A bloody nightmare!'

'Tell me everything, Fred. How did it happen?'

Maxim's voice was calm. There was no anger, but he wanted to know. The farmer looked up at Jonathan Maxim, someone he had come to regard almost as a surrogate son, but someone who, if all the rumours and gossip were true, could be an extremely dangerous man, a man who had killed. Fred Denby sobbed as he told his tale.

CHAPTER 32   MARCH THE FIRST (AGAIN)

March the first started off like many other days for Fred Denby. He woke at seven o'clock, got straight out of bed and, after a hearty breakfast and a good look at his phone app to assess today's racing, got his two border collies out of the outbuilding they had been locked in for the night. The dogs knew this routine. He fed them a tin of dogfood each and discarded the empty tins behind his garage.

'Right lads,' was his signal for the collies to race each other to the thirty-acre field behind the farmhouse. The one hundred sheep in there did not belong to Fred, neither did the fifty fattening bullocks in the adjacent field. The livestock were Keith Clarkson's at Hill Farm, over towards Hubberholme, who paid Fred on a monthly basis to provide extra grazing land. Winter was just about over now, and the grass was starting to take off. Fred kept an eye on the cattle and sheep for Keith and gave them food supplements as required.

'It keeps me ticking over,' was the phrase he used.

It was an ideal arrangement, some money coming in, but not much work. Soon it would be lambing time, a month of chaos that Fred would leave to his neighbour.

After walking the dogs, he returned to the farmhouse, letting the collies roam around the farmyard as they pleased. They happily sat to attention when their master left in the green Rover for his daily trip to Buckden. There he collected a few supplies from the corner shop along with the Racing Post. The rest of Fred's morning consisted of studying the form, sat at his living room table, eventually placing a myriad of small bets online using his smartphone app. As usual, he had left his backdoor open and, every now and then, the dogs would wander in to see what he was up to, and to be fed a biscuit or two.

At twelve o'clock on the dot, Fred went through to his kitchen to make himself lunch. He wasn't good at looking after himself, after being so reliant on his wife for all those years, and today was sausages. So fixed was his routine that the dogs, too, knew that today was sausages and patiently sat waiting for their share of the spoils.

Fred's afternoon was spent watching his horses underperform on the box, resulting in a forty quid loss.

'No apple today,' he said to the collies stretched out in front of the television.

After a snack tea and another walk out with the dogs, he locked them in the outbuilding. At around seven-thirty, to a crescendo of barking, Fred headed off in the Rover for Cray. It was only a mile and a half, and he could have walked, but he never did.

Less than ten minutes later, Fred Denby strode happily into The Lion's empty bar room and shouted across to Terry, the landlord.

'Pint of John Smiths, Terry. It'll be one of many so just tot them up as I go along.'

Terry was used to this. Fred was probably his most regular of regulars.

'Horses not done too well today, Fred?'

'Bloody useless. Just like backing donkeys, although I've seen some donkeys run faster on Scarborough beach!'

The banter continued as the landlord pulled the pint and Fred took his usual seat in his usual corner. He whiled away the time analysing the Racing Post app on his phone, still puzzling as to why such good horses had run so badly, and, by eight-fifteen, had downed three pints and was staring lovingly at a small glass of whisky, ready to savour it more slowly.

Fred heard a car door slam and seconds later a well-dressed middle-aged man walked purposefully into the room, striding across to the bar.

'A glass of coke, please barman,' he said to Terry.

'Canadian?' asked the landlord.

The man smiled.

'No, sir, from the States.'

Fred put his phone down on the table next to his whisky in order to pay attention. He could not recall an American ever being in the pub, let alone in a suit in March in walking country. The man glanced around the almost empty room, as if looking for somewhere to sit, before continuing.

'I'm trying to find a relative of mine. He's staying at a Scargill Cottage. Do you know it?'

'Ah, yes,' said Terry, 'up the hill from here. You turn right just down from the pub then right again after a climb of a mile or so. It's easy to spot. Tall conifers.'

Just then, four people noisily came through the pub entrance door carrying suitcases and haversacks, clearly having some argument about the Triangle Walk.

'Excuse me,' said Terry, 'I must see to my guests. I've been expecting them to arrive for the past hour or so.'

With that, the landlord left the bar and crossed the room to welcome the two young couples. After much smiling all five left to sort out accommodation for the night.

The American looked across at the Yorkshire farmer and walked over to his table.

'You know the area well?' he said, offering a smile.

'Very,' said Fred Denby, instinctively cautious and suspicious of the man.

'So, out of here, turn right, up the hill and look for tall conifers. That'll get me to Scargill Cottage?'

'That's right,' said Fred, 'but it'll do you no good.'

'Why not?'

'Well, I heard you say you're looking for a relative.'

'So?' came the quick reply.

'So,' said Fred, 'you won't find him there. There's nobody living in Scargill Cottage. It's empty, has been for at least six months.'

'Sure about that?'

'I live at Scargill Farm, just past it. Of course, I'm sure.'

The man nodded and turned away.

Fred frowned at him as he walked to the door. By the time that the American had started his car, Fred was watching from a window. He saw the car turn right and, for no reason that he could explain, began to panic. This American didn't look like anyone that Jonathan Maxim would have anything to do with. No friend, but he could be an enemy. All this was instinct to the farmer, admittedly after three pints and a whisky just downed in one. He must warn Jonathan. He stared at his phone and then realised that he had no idea of his number. The sixty-year-old farmer rushed out of the pub, as best he could, got in his Rover and set off in pursuit, with not the faintest idea of what he was going to do.

Fred drove slowly up the climb out of Cray. He was too nervous and affected by drink to go any faster. He would go to the cottage, to act as a witness and see that nothing happened to Jonathan. Perhaps that MI5 bloke would be there, anyway. Fred was making very little sense to himself. As he rounded the final bend before the conifers came into view, a poor view in darkness but aided by headlights and a full moon, he was surprised to see a car parked on the left, on the grass verge fifty yards or so past the entrance to the driveway. He immediately switched off his ignition and coasted to a halt a few yards behind the American's car.

He got out of the Rover and pushed the door to, noiselessly. Seeing no-one in the other car, he walked slowly back to the driveway entrance, panic hitting him when he heard movement from within the conifers, in front of him to his right. Instinct made him clutch his father's flick knife in his righthand pocket, a knife he had carried about his person every day for almost thirty years. As he pushed his way between two trees, he saw the outline of a man with his back to him facing the lit-up cottage two hundred yards away. Was it bravery that got the better of Fred, or just the alcohol?

'What the hell are you up to?' he shouted.

The figure whipped round and, before Fred had any time to react, he found himself pushed up against a tree, held by the throat, with a revolver pointed at his forehead.

'So, nobody lives in Scargill Cottage!' spat the American, recognising Fred in the moonlight.

The man took a step backwards and removed something from his pocket with his left hand. He held it up in front of the farmer's face.

'Look at this photograph. Tell me. Who's in there?'

'It's too dark. I can't see it properly,' Fred blurted out, petrified.

The man cocked his revolver.

'Look again!' he shouted.

Fred threw his left hand upwards. There was a loud explosion in his left ear as the gun went off and spun to the ground. The American's right fist was about to club the farmer over the head when there was a click, the flick knife blade sprang to its full extent, and Fred stuck it into the man's rib cage. As the man twisted away the knife broke, leaving the handle still clutched in the farmer's right hand. Yelping with pain, the American picked up the revolver. As he raised it to fire again, he was hit by a single swinging blow to his right temple, a punch thrown in sheer terror. He dropped spread-eagled to the ground, lifeless.

The farmer stood, panic stricken, struggling to breathe, chest heaving, staring at his still-clenched left fist.

'Christ, what have I done!' he shouted at himself.

He looked towards the cottage and saw a dark figure, half-lit by the security lights, running left into the wood.

The unfit overweight farmer turned and ran. Within forty-five seconds he was back in the Rover with the engine running. He put his foot on the accelerator and frantically spun the back wheels in the mud as he turned the car around. He could not go back to the farm. That would have condemned him as the guilty man. As he sped downhill towards Cray, his terrified mind searched for somewhere to run to. His brother lived only thirty miles away. No, that would be stupid too. The man who gambled every day, decided to gamble. Just before he got to Cray, he turned off his headlights and put his foot hard down on the clutch pedal. Silently, he freewheeled through the village and round the corner onto the main road. He was less than a hundred yards from The Lion. He took his foot off the clutch and edged forwards slowly to park the Rover opposite the pub, praying for the luck he needed. He left the car and slowly walked across to The Lion as calmly as he could, thinking of what he was going to say to Terry. He entered and gazed around. The room was empty.

'Bloody hell!' he thought.

He went to the bar and poured himself three glasses of whisky. Terry was used to Fred helping himself. He always paid, eventually. He took the drinks over to his usual table and drank two of the whiskies, putting the two empty glasses on the table with the third ready to drink. His empty glasses from earlier in the evening were still there! He sat down.

It was ten o'clock when the landlord came back into the bar, having given the four walkers platefuls of fish and chips after settling them into their rooms and nattering away for ages about their journey north and the Triangle Walk.

'Eh, Fred,' he shouted, 'don't forget to pay for those before you go.'

Fred Denby opened his eyes and yawned.

'Will do, Terry,' he replied. 'Can't seem to find my car keys though. I'll just have this whisky.'

Terry shook his head and went through to the breakfast area to set the tables for the morning. When he checked on Fred at eleven o'clock, the farmer was quietly snoring.

CHAPTER 33   THE END OF MAY

It had taken Fred Denby the best part of an hour to tell Jonathan Maxim what happened on that fateful day when alcohol, and his friendship with this strange young man, who throughout sat staring at the farmer without interruption, had got the better of him. At the end of his tale Fred was a nervous wreck, drenched in sweat, his fingers twitching with fear, unable to gauge Jonathan's reaction, because there was none.

Then, suddenly, there was silence, yet still there was no response. Seconds passed before the farmer asked:

'What do you think, Jon?'

Maxim nodded.

'You were lucky, Fred. That American was dangerous. You were very lucky.'

'What are you going to do, Jon?'

'What do you mean, Fred?'

'Well, I've killed someone. Should I confess to the police? Are you going to tell them?'

Jonathan's expression was one of dumbfounded amazement.

'Tell the police! No Fred. The American would have killed you. You were defending yourself. I've killed people who were trying to kill me. It's the right thing to do. No Fred. Well done.'

The farmer was shocked at Maxim's view of morality.

'Then, is there any more to be said, or do I just get on with things?'

'Yes, Fred, you just get on with things. Forget it ever happened. Mind you, as I said, you were lucky. That puny flick knife of yours didn't kill him. You got his right lung, which would have stung a bit, but it must have been the punch, from what Mister Tanner and the police said. Ever been in the Army, Fred?'

The farmer shook his head.

'Anyway, impressive, Fred. One punch and he was dead as a dodo.'

Jonathan sniggered.

'I know I shouldn't tell you, now that I work on classified stuff for the Government, but they think that a professional hitman, a Russian, did it. Funny, eh!'

He sniggered again, Fred staring open-mouthed.

'Well, time for me to go home. I still have my annoying GPS chip, but I am free now, Fred. I will be staying here forever, a few fields away from my friend and only three miles from my sister. Thanks for a smashing afternoon.'

Jonathan Maxim got out of his chair and held up his right hand as a parting gesture. Out in the Spring sunshine he got on his quadbike and accelerated away out of the farmyard to the accompaniment of barking.

He turned left and slowly made his way down the road before suddenly deciding to turn right and over the small rise along the path that led to the Triangle Walk. He braked to a halt at the view from the edge of his world. Before him stretched Wharfedale and, as always, he fixed his eyes on Buckden and the whitewashed pub in the distance, where his twin sister would be thinking of him.

He began to mull over everything that Fred had told him. It would be their secret. No-one else would know, not even Mister MI5. He laughed to himself and thought about what was hidden behind the wooden panel in his mother's bedroom, the revolver and the photograph. No, Mister MI5 would never know that they were there, nor who John Donnelly had come to kill. The photograph showed two men, side by side, smiling in the Iraqi sunshine years before. Those two men were Michael Maxim and the man who had run his covert ops, including the one in Northern Ireland, that man being David Tanner.

'You see, Mister Tanner,' said Jonathan Maxim to himself, 'nobody wanted to kill me, they wanted to kill you.'

He smiled to himself, turned the quadbike around, and headed home to Scargill Cottage.

Printed in Great Britain
by Amazon